Oedipus in
Brooklyn
and Other Stories

Oedipus in Brooklyn

and Other Stories

BLUME LEMPEL

Translated from the Yiddish by
Ellen Cassedy and
Yermiyahu Ahron Taub

MANDEL VILAR PRESS / DRYAD PRESS

This book is typeset in Bembo on 11.5 over 15.5
Book design by Sandy Rodgers
Cover art, "Innocence Reflected," by Fran Forman
Photographs of Blume Lempel courtesy of Paul Lempel

Library of Congress Cataloging-in-Publication Data

Names: Lempel, Blume, author. | Cassedy, Ellen, translator. | Taub, Yermiyahu
    Ahron, translator.
Title: Oedipus in Brooklyn & other stories / by Blume Lempel ; translated
    from the Yiddish by Ellen Cassedy and Yermiyahu Ahron Taub.
Other titles: Oedipus in Brooklyn and other stories
Description: Simsbury, Connecticut : Mandel Vilar Press ; Takoma Park,
    Maryland : Dryad Press, [2016] | The first eleven stories in this volume
    were published in Yiddish in "A rege fun emes" (A moment of truth), by
    Blume Lempel (Tel Aviv: I.L. Peretz Publishing House, 1981). The second
    eleven stories were published in Yiddish in "Balade fun a kholem" (Ballad
    of a dream), by Blume Lempel (Tel Aviv: Israel Book Publishing House,
    1986). | Includes bibliographical references and index.
Identifiers: LCCN 2016035817 (print) | LCCN 2016036370 (ebook) |
    ISBN 9781942134251 (hardcover : alk. paper) | ISBN 9781942134213
    (pbk. : alk. paper) | ISBN 9781942134220 (E-book)
Subjects: LCSH: Short stories, Yiddish. | LCGFT: Short stories.
Classification: LCC PJ5129.L4175 A6 2016 (print) | LCC PJ5129.L4175
    (ebook) | DDC 839/.134--dc23
LC record available at https://lccn.loc.gov/2016035817

Mandel Vilar Press / 19 Oxford Court, Simsbury, Connecticut 06070
www.americasforconservation.org / www.mvpress.org

Dryad Press / P.O. Box 11233, Takoma Park, Maryland 20913
www.dryadpress.com

ACKNOWLEDGMENTS

The first eleven stories in this volume were published in Yiddish in *A rege fun emes* (*A Moment of Truth*), by Blume Lempel (Tel Aviv: I.L. Peretz Publishing House, 1981). The second eleven stories were published in Yiddish in *Balade fun a kholem* (*Ballad of a Dream*), by Blume Lempel (Tel Aviv: Israel Book Publishing House, 1986). These stories were translated with the kind permission of Blume Lempel's son, Paul Lempel.

"Pastorale" appeared in Yiddish in *Di goldene keyt* (Tel Aviv: No. 122, 1987). "The Fate of the Yiddish Writer" appeared in Yiddish in *Yidishe kultur* (New York: Vol. 48, November/December 1986). "The Death of My Aunt," translated by Ellen Cassedy, and "Neighbors over the Fence," translated by Ellen Cassedy and Yermiyahu Ahron Taub, appeared previously in slightly different form in *Pakn Treger*, the magazine of the Yiddish Book Center. "Pastorale," translated by Ellen Cassedy and Yermiyahu Ahron Taub, appeared in *KIN: Journal of Literary Translation* (Ottawa: Issue 8, April 2016). "The Little Red Umbrella," translated by Ellen Cassedy and Yermiyahu Ahron Taub, appeared in *The Brooklyn Rail: In Translation* (Brooklyn, NY: April 2016).

The Hadassah-Brandeis Institute and the Sonya Staff Foundation provided financial support for the translation project.

TABLE OF CONTENTS

Introduction / ix

Even the Heavens Tell Lies / 3

Pachysandra / 13

The Death of My Aunt / 21

Images on a Blank Canvas / 31

Neighbors over the Fence / 41

The Debt / 49

My Friend Ben / 55

Oedipus in Brooklyn / 63

Cousin Claude / 75

A Yiddish Poet in Paris / 87

The Power of a Melody / 101

Yosele / 105

The Bag Lady of Seventh Avenue / 115

En Route to Divorce / 121

The Little Red Umbrella / 131

Her Last Dance / 143

Waiting for the Ragman / 155

The Twin Sisters / 167

A Little Song for a Jewish Soul / 175

The Invented Brother / 179

A Snowstorm in Summerland / 189

Yosemite Park /199

Pastorale / 207

The Fate of the Yiddish Writer (essay) / 215

Translators' Acknowledgments / 221

About the Translators / 224

INTRODUCTION

Blume Lempel (1907-1999) was a remarkably original storyteller — unique in her style, her narrative strategies, and her subject matter. With their lyrical, idiosyncratic imagery, her sentences often evoke an unsettling blend of splendor and menace. Many of the storylines are characterized by restless flashbacks, jarring juxtapositions, uneven pacing, and abrupt endings. "I like to start at the end and work backward," she said. "Or start in the middle. Or begin with some strange subject and then change the character entirely and start all over again."

Lempel's narratives migrate between past and present, Old World and New, dream and reality. Some stories resemble collages whose carefully arranged fragments reverberate against one another, wandering from modern-day New York to prewar Poland, bedtime story to passionate romance, old age dementia to girlhood dreams. The boundaries between real and unreal can be fragile and permeable. Cosmic landscapes rub up against domestic scenes. Multiple time periods coexist on a single page.

Lempel was drawn to subjects that were seldom explored by other writers in Yiddish in her time — abortion, prostitution, women's erotic imaginings, incest. With rare acuity, she explores her characters' inner lives; faced with impossible choices, they tend to resist grand, heroic action. Instead, they engage in a struggle with memory, mood, and shifts in consciousness as they confront the madness of history and sometimes seek to fend off the oncoming madness of the self. Often they are propelled by encounters with powerful natural forces, which can be feverish and erotically tinged or full of horror.

Blume Lempel's life traced a trajectory from Eastern Europe to Paris to New York. Born Blume Leye Pfeffer in Khorostkiv, a small town in what was then Galicia (now western Ukraine), she grew up in what she described as "a white-washed room by the banks of a river that had no name." Her father was a butcher; her mother read novels and was considered learned by the townspeople. For several years, Blume attended a religious school for girls and a Hebrew folk school, and at times a tutor came to the house; still, her formal education was minimal.

As a child, she recalled, "I didn't write at all; I only dreamed of writing." Throughout her girlhood years, however, she was storing up sights and sounds that she would later weave into her stories — images of wheat fields shimmering in the sun, boots covered with dust from the mill, beggars and pickpockets in the market square, the sounds of Hasidic melodies, the springtime concert of the frogs, fiery Zionist speeches.

When Blume was twelve, her mother died, her father remarried, and she was pressed into service as a housekeeper and nursemaid for the new couple and their young child. In 1929, at 22, she left home intending to become a pioneer in Palestine. On the way, she stopped off in Paris to visit her brother Yisroel — he had fled Khorostkiv after being arrested for revolutionary activity and settled in the vibrant Jewish immigrant neighborhood of Belleville. Blume was captivated by the City of Light and abandoned her pioneer plans. She attended night school, began writing poetry, and found a job in the fur industry, where she met Lemel (Leon) Lempel. The couple married and had two children.

As Hitler's power grew, the family managed to secure immigration papers and sailed for New York in 1939. Blume had been exceptionally happy in Paris and had every intention of returning, but it was not to be. The Lempels settled permanently in New York, first in Brooklyn and later in Long Beach, off the south shore of Long Island, on the Atlantic Ocean.

Soon after arriving in the U.S., Lempel began to write short stories. Her first published work, "*Muter un tokhter*" ("Mother and Daughter"), appeared in the Yiddish daily newspaper *Der tog* in 1943 under the pseudonym Rokhl Halperin, the name of an aunt. A few years later, the New York newspaper *Morgn frayhayt* serialized her panoramic novel of prewar Paris, *Tsvishn tsvey veltn* (*Between Two Worlds*), which features a romance between a Jewish woman and a Nazi. It was published in English in 1954 as *Storm over Paris*.

These promising literary beginnings were stymied, however, as Lempel's home responsibilities increased. Her aunt Rokhl moved in, a third child was born, and an orphaned nephew joined the family. More than these obligations, though, it was the devastating news from across the Atlantic that brought her writing to a standstill. Her father's wife and their young son, she learned, had been killed by the Nazis; her father then set fire to the family home and hanged himself. Her brother, who had joined the French resistance, was arrested and shot in Lyon. Increasingly despondent, she felt "paralyzed within a self-imposed prison," she wrote later. "The years went by, many desolate, fruitless years."

A turning point came when a friend suggested she try writing about the catastrophic events that were consuming her. Taking up her pen once more, she discovered a new literary calling: to "speak for those who could no longer speak, feel for those who could no longer feel, immerse myself in their unlived lives, their sorrows, their joys, their struggle and their death."

Having left Europe on the eve of World War II, Lempel did not directly experience the roundups, mass executions, and concentration camps of the Holocaust. She offers glimpses of these, while powerfully exploring the experience of displacement, flight, and adaptation, as well as the special burden of remembrance and retribution, grief and guilt, carried by the living.

By the beginning of the 1970's, Lempel's poems and short stories were being published regularly in Yiddish periodicals in the U.S. and abroad, including *Zayn, Tsukunft, Undzer eygn vort, Yidishe kultur, Forverts, Yidisher kemfer,* and *Algemayner dzhurnal* (New York); *Khezhbn* (California); *Di goldene keyt, Bay zikh, Naye tsaytung,* and *Yisroel shtime* (Israel); *Letste nayes* (Australia); *Undzer veg* (Paris); and *Dorem afrike* (South Africa). Many of her stories were collected in two volumes published in Tel Aviv, Israel: *A rege fun emes* (*A Moment of Truth*) in 1981 and *Balade fun a kholem* (*Ballad of a Dream*) in 1986.

Over the years, Lempel received numerous Yiddish literary prizes and became part of the worldwide Yiddish literary network. As the number of Yiddish literary writers diminished, they sustained one another through constant communication. She was fortunate to win support from the renowned poet Abraham Sutzkever, the founder and editor of *Di goldene keyt*. In Tel Aviv, the poets Binem Heller and Yankev-Tsvi Shargel helped shepherd her volumes to publication. She engaged in warm correspondence with the writers Chava Rosenfarb and Malka Heifetz Tussman; her personal papers contain letters from numerous critics and fans, including such literary figures as Chaim Grade and Yonia Fain.

Over the course of her career, Lempel attended writing classes and read widely, but she remained fiercely self-directed. While her decision to write in Yiddish was a carefully considered choice, integral to her literary mission, she did not feel part of a literary "school" or trend in any language. Asked by an interviewer about writers who had influenced her, she could not cite any. "I feel I don't borrow from anyone," she said.

Old age did not stop Lempel's creative output. When her husband Leon died in 1986, Blume wrote in a poem that she had "nothing more to tell/ nothing more to say." In fact, however, her stories and poems continued to appear in the 1990's, when she was well into her eighties.

Blume Lempel died in 1999 in Long Beach, New York, at the age of 93. Her extraordinary stories live on.

Ellen Cassedy
Yermiyahu Ahron Taub

A Note about Transliteration

For words of Hebrew and Yiddish origin that have been accepted into English, we follow the spelling found in Webster's Dictionary. For other Yiddish words, including those of Hebrew origin, in most cases we follow the system established by the YIVO Institute for Jewish Research. Names of cultural figures and place names generally follow the forms found in the Library of Congress Authority File.

Oedipus in Brooklyn

and Other Stories

EVEN THE HEAVENS TELL LIES

I was not born mute. My silence is not genetic. Something jammed up inside me and I stopped speaking — when and why, I no longer remember. I listen to what people say, but I cannot answer them. In my mind, I speak to the shadows that populate my world, to the wind and the rain — and to the cat living outside my door. The cat is the one who insists on the separation, not me. Innately stubborn, she always declines when I invite her to share the shelter of my four walls. I don't try to coax her into my friendly lap, there to nap and there, like Hamlet, perchance to dream. Within the muddle of her feline brain, a thousand tangled nerves warn her to stay away from people. I respect the attitude of her kind and admire her willpower. It takes strength to refuse a warm corner when the temperature drops below zero and the snow covers her accustomed footpaths. Her courage and self-sacrifice touch me to the depths, where my pain is buried. I start to laugh, softly at first, under my breath — a queer, choked laughter — and then, as if I've touched an electric current, my shoulders begin to quiver and my knees give out. I see stars, and my head spins — a sign that the pain is rising, threatening to flood my consciousness with its lava. At that point I know not to wait any longer and I stick in the needle.

People wonder why I never cry. The doctors think that if I did, the walls of my resistance might crumble and I might be able to speak again. They've even tried hurting me physically, but the pain only made me laugh.

And yet I remember that I used to cry, to speak, to tell and retell the stories I used to hear on winter nights around the stove. I'd brush the mildew from the old pages and arrange them lovingly on memory's shelf. In my mind, fantastic Edens bloomed and white birds spread their wings to guard the boundary between good and evil.

Growing up, I had no reason to doubt the established order. Enclosed within my father's words and my mother's tears, the world came to me as a finished product, and I accepted its colors and nuances as part of the natural arrangement of things. Just as the sun rose every morning behind our barn and set every evening behind the tree that my father pointed to, so I stayed within the picture frame, walking in the light, avoiding the shadows, never straying beyond the borders. The house where I was born and grew up was my personal fortress. Over the walls a roof and over the roof a sky — a frame atop a frame, double insurance against malevolent forces that lay in wait beyond. When my father shut the gate every evening, I was certain that nothing harmful would befall me. The peasants on the other side of the river might be wounding one another with knives, the wind might be howling and the forest black as hell, but I didn't worry. I had no doubt that what lay within the frame could resist all the dark powers.

Maybe it was the strength of my belief in that order, in the bookkeeper's columns of good and bad, in words, in the talk that sustained those concepts — perhaps this was why I ceased to speak.

When I lived with the squirrel in the forest, speech was unnecessary. From her, I learned the art of survival. With eyes open and mouth shut, I followed in her tracks, learning to beware of the slightest rustle, the tiniest vibration from miles away. Life there sharpened my senses until I could distinguish between prey and predator and identify animals and people by scent alone.

She led me to trees laden with nuts. In that region the squirrels were plump and well-fed. Once, lightning set fire to a tree and incinerated a whole family of them. I remember the taste of those singed creatures. The grease trickled down as I gnawed the marrow of their charred bones. I felt the power of their extinguished lives filling my veins with strength. New energy welled up inside me. I felt as strong as Samson and left my forest bunker ready to take on the murderers and finish them off with a single blow.

In such limpid moments, the scent of my mother's body would come to me, her skin smelling of noodles fried in oil and honey. How good it felt to cry on her breast! "Children's tears never go to waste," she used to say. "Innocent tears find their way to the Throne of God."

I did not cry my last tears before God. I cried before Temke, our peasant neighbor. I wanted him to bury my parents, and so I cried before him. I never cried again.

I don't know how I managed to bury my parents in the Jewish cemetery. Today this holy ground is covered with cement. A cultural center has been erected, with a red roof and playgrounds and peaceful gardens where Temke and his fellow lowlifes can enjoy themselves. There was a time when I believed that only from this cemetery could the souls of my parents ascend to the loftiest heights imaginable.

After the last roundup, when my parents were killed, I left Temke's barn and went into the woods. The darkness that had once frightened me became my protector, sheltering and concealing me. The wind mingled my scent with the smells of the forest. The rain washed away my footprints. I followed the animals and kept away from people. The wind brought me the smell of berries, a dead bird, the rotten carcass of a half-devoured creature. Under cover of night, propelled by hunger, I pursued these scents. The forest took me in without tears, without words, receiving me with indifference, a naked, frank, and savage truth — one single truth for the worm in the grass, the rabbit in the thicket, tree, star, nuts, and me.

In such profound connection, I would close my eyes without fear or sorrow. As I merged with the impersonal ways of nature, my body would forsake me — until the wind stirred and I descended once again to my hiding place.

When I was discovered and returned to life among people, I was unable to utter a word. I thought I'd become deaf to human speech. But that was wishful thinking. In fact, I didn't want to hear about the enormity of the disaster. Instead, I looked for answers with my eyes. I scrabbled in the garbage with my fingernails. I tasted the dust, pawed at the stones. I sought a path to the house where I was born, the room where my cradle once stood. I looked for the barn behind which the sun would set. I sniffed for my mother's honeyed scent in the mountains of ash. Even the sky was gone. The horizon had burned away, leaving no center, no foothold, no answer, no purpose.

I searched and searched until the pain exploded, and then I began to laugh. I was taken to a doctor who peered into my eyes, my heart, and my soul, and declared that I needed to rest. Total rest and good care, he said, would calm my nerves and make me normal once more.

I'm sure he meant no harm, this Jewish doctor in his Russian uniform. But the word "normal" provoked me, touching a nerve at the root of my illness. Long-sealed sluices of buried pain burst open. Waves of molten wrath, shame, and murdered hope flooded over the banks, accompanied by spasmodic laughter. I laughed until the flames smothered my breath and I lost consciousness. It was then that the doctor administered the first injection.

I found it difficult to leave the cemetery — not only the one now covered with cement, but also the burial ground of my orderly childhood world. After the efficient destruction, all that remained were chimneys and orphaned walls. I could not bear to leave these, to part with the mound of rubbish and the earthen bench where my friend Rosa's home once stood. No doubt that bench remembered the Yiddish songs we sang there — and even if the bench did not remember, I could not forget. Nor could I forget Reyzye Paltiels with her gold tooth, through which she filtered her rippling octaves. Reyzye was the only girl in town who could sing "Aida" with all the trills, like a diva. Her exquisite love songs ascended like prayers to the house high on the mountain where Yosele lived. She and I both knew Yosele was standing by the back gate, looking out through a crack. He climbed the towering heights of her song and fluttered on fantasy wings, soaring on the tones of her Song of Songs without regard for the abyss that yawned below. Yosele knew that his father, a wealthy dry goods merchant, would never consent to a match with the daughter of a wagon driver. But Reyzye had her own ideas. She heeded the urgency of her feelings and the power of the kiss she had shared with Yosele in the grove under cover of night.

The apple trees are still standing in Reyzye's orchard. Perhaps they remember the loving couple's last kiss, or the tear from Reyzye's brown eyes, or the sigh that trembled with leaves in the wind.

I sit on the bench as the shadows gather around me. They sprawl at my feet and coil around my throat, my heart, my thoughts — and because I have nothing to say to them, I begin to laugh. I laugh against my will, against my better judgment. I laugh until I stick in the needle and try to convince myself that I'm normal.

The shadows come and go, but my friend Rosa is always beside me. We speak without words, like the river at the foot of the mountain that flows on as though nothing has changed. We do not speak of the torn garments of bereavement that separate us, nor of the sea of blood nor the mountain of ash.

At the foot of the mountain on the other side of the river, the fields extend as far as the eye can see, and the ripe wheat waves in the wind as if yesterday had never happened. Geese and ducks swim in the river, filling the air with their brash cries. In the evening, they shake the water off their wings and return to their nests. The peasant women who have spent all day with the flax lay their sheaves in the shallow water and cover them with mud. They wash their feet and make their way toward home. On that side of the river lies the village with no past. Smoke winds from the peasant chimneys as supper is prepared. Mothers rock their children to sleep. Under one of those thatched roofs lives Temke. In his barn he keeps our cows and the horse I used to ride. For the privilege of spending the winter in that barn, I turned over all our belongings. He took Mother's gold chain and Father's watch. In the special Passover dish that was my mother's pride and joy, Temke now cooks his unkosher delicacies.

I say nothing to Rosa about all this, nor do I tell her that during the winter I spent in Temke's barn, he raped me. With Rosa I speak in a silent tongue, heart to heart. We gaze upon the slender flaxen threads that drift by like thoughts, floating in the air like the nerves of mutilated bodies that refuse to die. Night falls, but we have nowhere to go. We watch the birds rising from the fields. We do not curse the fields, or the black earth rich with the blood of our murdered world. We don't talk about today. We immerse ourselves in the past, in girlish dreams, in the crushes we'll pursue when we're as old as Reyzye Paltiels.

We talk about Bumke, the boy with the shock of black hair. Rosa still believes he visits our street because he's after her, but I know that I'm the one he wants. I see him even now in the withered grove. The wind plays with his tousled hair, and I feel his eyes on me and grow hot. I feel he knows what Temke did to me. Perhaps he thinks I've been defiled. I can't blame him. He was not in the forest. And after all, he's still so young. He will never be older than fifteen.

We talk late into the night, until morning. We talk and we talk, about Israel, about the pioneers who are now there and those who are planning to go. We burn with the passion of speeches made in the Great Synagogue. Even if we can't grasp the situation with the British, we believe the fiery words of the speakers. We're part of the fire sweeping through our world, the lava in the mouth of the volcano. We believe in the blue-and-white flag and the Hebrew songs, the agricultural training and the survival of our people. We believe!

When I crossed the ocean, I carried with me the habit of speaking to the shadows, and it became my way of life. I look up at the stars that were extinguished long ago. For me they still shine with the first fire of creation. I don't care that the heavens tell lies. I accept the fantasy along with the fact. I'm not looking for truth. I'm seeking the faith that I've lost, a way out of chaos, a place where my broken self can put down roots. I know the evil powers that live within people and make no attempt to cloak them in pretty words. I don't separate myself from the community, but I live on the sidelines, like a stranger in my own world. I live with the snakes and scorpions, with the black leeches in my brain, in my blood.

I live with the garden in my backyard. Among the stones I carried with me, flowers grow. I refer to them by the names of those who are no more. They burn like memorial candles, each in its season. My parents, who were killed in winter, emerge from the snow, their tart red berries reaching up like blood-soaked fingers. I watch as the hungry birds peck at the berries one by one. My mother's white fingers seem to hold out fruit for the birds. I like to think she enjoys having them eat from her hands.

The first bloom that breaks through the winter crust is named Rosa. She appears as a narcissus, white, slender, and shy. The snow may lie at her feet, but she tolerates the bitter weather, bestowing the rich perfumes of her pure soul upon the wind and holding her head high, stretching up with youthful exhilaration. Sometimes she lasts for a day, sometimes for a week, but the bulb stays planted deep in the earth. She will return, and she knows I will be waiting.

My summer flowers, on the other hand, have no fixed identities. They change their character day by day, according to my mood. When the sky is blue, the gladiolus laughs with my cousin Gitl's sensuous mirth. The pink goblet with its red rim reminds me of Gitl's half-parted lips. Always eager to be fruitful and multiply, at twenty she was already the mother of two sets of twins. Whenever she was nursing a child, her mind flooded with intoxicating notions. She lowered her gray eyes, ashamed to raise them lest her thoughts be revealed. Perhaps she asked God to forgive her for feeling such heated desire for her husband. It was said that at the very end she was pregnant again. A German put a bullet in her belly and left her lying in the street with her guts spilling out. The sight was so unsettling that the peasants crossed themselves in fear on their way to church that Sunday. In my mind I lift her up and carry her far away from human eyes. Surely if a wolf came upon her in the forest he would devour her. A cannibal would make a feast of her. Yet her ultra-civilized murderer left her lying in the street to show the world what he could do.

The shadows slink around me as I sit in my garden. A smile, a gesture, swims into memory. They are not numbers but living people, each one unique. In the rich soil of my garden, their severed lives are flourishing. Pansies with violet eyes, blue forget-me-nots, red poppies like congealed blood, white roses choked by murderous parasitic vines — side by side with yesterday, a today is blooming. Often I feel that a tomorrow, too, is growing.

Whenever I recall a particular face, I plant a flower. I don't pamper my blooms with synthetic food. They must cope with the raw elements. Free from illusions, self-aware, they rely on no one but themselves. Soaking up hot sunshine and plenteous rain, hail and hurricane, they know the art of adaptation and survival.

Sometimes, when storms fail to arrive and the thorns on my roses turn limp and passive, a fear overtakes me. In my desperation I summon a storm of my own, awakening shadows with my mute wailing, my wild laughter. I laugh and I storm, and it seems to me that the wind storms with me.

PACHYSANDRA

Everyone who knew Pachysandra knew that she talked to herself. Yet her face never betrayed the slightest hint of what she was talking about. Her expression remained hard, closed, the brick-colored skin drawn taut over her cheeks, her eyes shaded by the brim of the straw hat she never removed.

As soon as she opened her eyes in the morning and remembered who and where she was, her lips began to move — not just with any words, but with verses from the Bible. The first verse that came to mind and fully penetrated her consciousness would stay with her all day long, to be recited over and over from morning to night.

Pachysandra did not select her own material. Biblical texts and images flooded her imagination, adapting themselves to her moods, which shifted in reaction to the weather, or to an argument with her son Tom, or to some distant pagan source whose origins she did not know and did not want to know.

Pachysandra believed in the holy patriarchs of the Old Testament.

She knew they were looking after her because they came without premeditation or prayer. They arose from the depths of her spirit, filling every corner of her room, settling on the bed, giving her advice on what to cook and what to eat. When she laughed, they laughed with her; when she cried, they cried, too. They embraced her like a trellis of roses, guarding and protecting her private world.

All day, while her mind was busy with this and that, the images were in motion. Figures appeared as if under a silver cloud. She saw Abraham's caravan on the edge of the desert and the matriarch Sarah, encircled by a retinue of maidservants and wrapped in white linen, riding side-saddle on a small donkey. Pachysandra couldn't see her face, but sensed her royal bearing, and with the utmost respect she chose not to peel away the swaths of fabric protecting her privacy. For each image, she had a corresponding verse. The images and the verses populated Pachysandra's world, which she tended in a special chamber of her being, minute as a pinhead and yet infinite.

Pachysandra saw parallels between Sarah's fortunes and her own. She too had rescued her only son from the butcher knife that he himself had sharpened. She too had crossed the river into a foreign land — and not just one river, but many rivers, many seas, until the very last wandering that brought her from South Carolina to cold, alien Brooklyn.

Pachysandra yearned for South Carolina. She missed the wide open universe, as wide and open as God had created it. Every morning when she went shopping for her son Tom, she made a detour through Prospect Park so that she could luxuriate in the scent of the grass, the trees, the water. She scolded the birds in the park if they refused the bread crumbs she'd set aside for them the previous evening.

"If I had any teeth, I wouldn't be tossing God's bread at you like this," she told them. "The Creator has already provided you with nuts from the trees and worms from the earth." Pachysandra carried the leftover crumbs to the river where the less finicky ducks quickly devoured them.

"How happy you are," she said to the ducks. "You have no worries or concerns. Your conscience doesn't bother you when you grab a morsel from another's mouth. You know nothing of sin, you live and laugh as if you'd never left the Garden of Eden nor eaten from the Tree of Knowledge. All's well with you, my little ones. Eat, eat, and enjoy."

Even as she spoke to the birds, the song inside her continued without interruption, seamlessly anchoring her to the spiritual world.

Sometimes Pachysandra forgot a word from the tract she was repeating. When this happened, she'd open her straw purse to touch the Bible that she always carried with her. The word would come to her immediately, pronounced in the quavering tones used by the preacher every Sunday morning in South Carolina.

Pachysandra tended the small plot of green that graced the entrance to the big apartment building where her son Tom was the superintendent. As she gardened, her mind often strayed to far-away South Carolina, where each drop of water was repaid with the blessing of abundance: golden corn and green peppers. There her life had taken root like a seed dropped in the earth. The rise and fall of her green days pursued her in her dreams. The faded images appeared the moment she fell asleep.

In her dreams she and Tom's father are still young. They pick cotton side by side in the sun-drenched fields. At the end of the day, they count how many bushels they've picked. Sometimes she dreams she's waiting for Tom's father in the high corn. All her limbs draw her toward him. He stands nearby, but is unable to see her. He looks past her into the distance. She feels his breath on her face, sees the sweat that has trickled into his eyes from under his wide-brimmed hat. He wipes his face with his torn shirt and flashes his white teeth, always ready to laugh.

His playful laughter flows out of the pillow, sometimes turning into lament. Wanting to console him, she searches for words to soothe his sorrow. She looks for her Bible, but can't find it — and when she does, all the pages are blank. In her younger days, truth be told, she knew very little about the Bible. She went to church only on the most important holidays. It was not until Tom's father was brought home dead that she began to pay attention to the preacher's sermons.

She used to sit on the wobbly rocking chair in the front room of her little house with the child at her breast, rocking back and forth in search of God. All the world stretched before her like a desert. With the child in her arms, like the Biblical Hagar before her, she searched for a spring where she could fill her jug. And the spring rose up before her. And she lifted her eyes and saw the great house on the other side of the tracks, beyond the grand garden where her mother had once worked. Now, Pachysandra arose early every day, took the boy by the hand, and went to the great house. Day in and day out, with the boy in tow, she did all that she was told. In the evening, she returned home to her ramshackle cottage by the open field.

The deep wounds left by Tom's father's death dried out under the southern sun. The years passed, and Tom grew tall and strong, the image of his father. Women chased after him. The one he chose to marry later came to betray him. She aroused in Tom the bad blood of his father, and this caused her, Pachysandra, to swear falsely.

Late in the evening in her rocking chair she would speak to God. She spoke to Him directly, without restraint. The mild breezes that knew all the secret pathways carried her prayers to the place where all heartfelt pleas must go. Even today, in Brooklyn, she lived by the grace of those heavens and by the blessing that pulsed in that brown earth.

When Tom decided to become a superintendent in Brooklyn, she brought with her a small box filled with that earth, dug from behind the old walnut tree where she and Tom's father used to meet. The tree hadn't produced any nuts for years. Spanish moss hung thickly on its branches, like faded mourning shawls on the heads of widows. Pachysandra placed the earth in the finely carved box that Tom's father had once given her filled with chocolate.

In her basement home in Brooklyn the little box sat on a private altar covered with a white tablecloth embroidered with colorful flowers. Beside it was a portrait of Mother Mary with the crucified Christ in her arms, and nearby an incense burner and the Bible, which she took out of her straw purse as soon as she came home.

When her heart was heavy, Pachysandra would kneel before the altar. Her eyes were hungry for a small patch of sky or the edge of a green field. But all she could see through her small basement window were feet, without faces or bodies, forever tramping back and forth. It seemed to Pachysandra that they wanted to crush her and bury her under the dust of the city until not the slightest trace remained of her past or of the mother who'd birthed her.

Tom, too, felt choked by the umbilical cord to which he was attached. Pachysandra saw him as the very incarnation of his father. He roared like his father and gnashed his teeth, and he, too, believed that God was a white man and that only through blood and fire would the black man find his place in the world.

Pachysandra listened to him talk. She rocked back and forth as he spoke, as if she were still sitting in her rocking chair in far-away South Carolina. A great pity overcame her when she considered her son's loneliness and his tormented, starved, and depleted soul. She longed to share with him the riches of her faith, the dream that couldn't be bought with money nor broadcast over television or transistor radio. She wanted to reveal her visions to him, but knew not to disclose this secret. Tom was sure to laugh at her. The patriarchs have no one better to visit than an old black maid from South Carolina, he'd mock.

Knowing what he would say, she kept the vision locked up inside, protecting it from eyes that looked but couldn't see and from hearts that couldn't feel. The tie was between her and her God, and she would carry the secret with her to the grave.

On her knees, Pachysandra looked beyond the crucifix to the night when Tom came home with a knife in hand, intent on killing his wife. He had just found out that she'd betrayed him. Pachysandra planted herself between them and grabbed the knife by the blade.

"Get out of the way," he shouted, "or I'll kill you both!"

"You're not going to kill anyone," Pachysandra answered.

Tom saw the blood gushing from his mother's hand and Myrtle, his wife, lying unconscious on the floor.

"Your wife is innocent," Pachysandra said. "I swear to you on the Holy Bible that an enemy has cooked up these false accusations to destroy you, just as your father was destroyed."

"My father defended his honor."

"Your father accepted a liar's word."

"Swear!" Tom roared.

"I swear!" she replied.

"On the open Bible?"

"On the open Bible!"

"On my father's honor?"

"On your father's honor."

Pachysandra placed her bloody hand on the Holy Book and swore an oath that she knew to be false.

That night Pachysandra sat in her rocking chair enveloped in darkness. She waited, hoping her punishment would come like a lightning bolt and strike her down on the spot. She waited for the gates of hell to open up and for devils to emerge with glowing tongs to roast her flesh, or for a snake to spring out of the grass, wrap itself around her neck and strangle her. She opened her heart and laid bare her soul to receive the punishment. She was prepared to pay with her own life for saving the life of her son.

Pachysandra closed her eyes. Cool sea breezes caressed her burning face, her bony hands, her bare feet. She drew her shawl tighter around her shoulders; her head sank to her breast. She saw the oleander tree that grew beside the little house, climbing like a ladder toward the vault of heaven. High above, on a lattice of roses, the figures were descending. One, two, three, four women clad in white. They stepped down the ladder and settled on the rungs and the ramp. They were quarreling over a matter she knew well.

"She desecrated God's word," said one.

"She conducted herself as a mother would," replied a second.

"She swore falsely."

"She saved her daughter-in-law from death and her son from eternal prison."

"She used God's word for falsehood."

"She acted like a mother."

"We are all mothers."

"Who can judge a mother's heart when her only son is being led to the sacrificial altar?"

"My twin sons were not bound for the altar, but I followed the dictates of my heart, not my mind."

"I bore ten sons and abandoned them all to their own fate."

Only the fourth one, the youngest, said nothing. She allowed her attendants to smooth out the folds of her white dress. Her head was bent low, and from the trembling of her shoulders it was clear that she was weeping.

To Pachysandra it seemed as if the hot tears of that veiled figure were running down her own face. She forced her eyes open, wanting to hold onto the dream, to run after the esteemed guests and offer them refreshment, perhaps something cold to drink and an ear of roasted corn. She longed to sit at their feet and listen to them argue. She would accept their judgment, whether good or bad. Around her the night was still and empty. She bent down and kissed the steps where the honored visitors had sat.

It was just a dream! a voice whispered, but Pachysandra did not want to hear. Instead, she listened to the rustle that their fine garments left behind in the air, and to the lament of the youngest and most beautiful of them all.

Pachysandra rose as if in a trance and saw that the heavens were parting. She was not surprised. Deep in her soul she knew that this was how it was meant to be. She made no attempt to understand the miracle. From the open heavens, a fiery arm reached out, sowing the vast field of the night sky with stars.

That night, at that moment, a spring burst open and holy words began to gush forth. Entire chapters of the Bible flooded over her. Her lips began to move. Words poured out as if from an overflowing jug. A choir of angels sang along with her.

All night, Pachysandra stood under the open skies. She didn't see a rainbow, but in the very core of her being she knew that that night she had signed a covenant with the Almighty. She would repeat the words of the Bible all the days of her life. The Bible would be the very essence of her life. Whenever the words welled up, God would protect her, both her and her son Tom.

THE DEATH OF MY AUNT

In the early hours after midnight, the telephone sounds altogether different — or so it seemed to me when the metallic jangle pounced like a thief that night, putting a swift end to my dreams and driving me out of bed. I ran down the long, dark corridor to the dining room and reached for the receiver.

"Yes?" I croaked, half asleep.

I couldn't catch who was on the line. "Who did you say is speaking?"

"The old age home on Howard Avenue," the voice said.

I felt for a chair and sat down. The spiders that nest in hidden places had come out into the open, tightening the loose strands of their webs with their thin, hairy legs. I clutched the receiver with both hands.

"Are you all right, Mrs. Lempel?" The feigned politeness was infuriating. I was tempted to ask whether he'd called at two o'clock in the morning just to find out how I was. But my throat closed up.

The voice on the other side of the night spoke again. "I'm sorry to say we have some sad news for you. Your aunt — your aunt, Rokhl Halperin, is no longer among the living."

The flush that had broken out all over my body turned to a chill, and then I was hot again. With the receiver still at my ear, I opened the window. A cold gust of wind swept over me. A car sped by. In the glow of the headlights I could see it was snowing. The grass around the house was already white.

"Mrs. Lempel?"

"Yes?"

"We'll be arranging for the funeral first thing in the morning. We'd like you to be here then."

I waited a moment. "When did it happen?"

"Saturday at five in the afternoon."

His cool demeanor made me want to scream, curse, draw blood. Why, why had they waited until two o'clock in the morning to call me? Why had they allowed her to die all alone?

"Mrs. Lempel, I can tell you're upset. I understand your position and I don't want to argue with you. But you must understand — "

I closed the window and tried to understand. Why was he calling on Sunday, when she'd suffered the first heart attack Thursday? From what he said, on Friday she'd improved a bit; then Saturday morning she'd had the second attack. She'd wrestled with the Angel of Death, kept up the fight till evening....

I couldn't listen any longer. I hung up the phone and went back to bed.

My husband and children had slept through it all. Why should I wake them now?

She'd waited for me, hoping I would come. Why on earth hadn't they called? Why had they done this to her, to me? Abruptly I sat up in bed. I wanted to call the home and scream: Murderers! Robbers!

To save the cost of a lousy phone call you shatter the lifelong dream of a poor old woman?

But instead of going to the telephone, I went to the window and parted the curtains. I looked out at the tree swaying in the wind. The snow had turned into a heavy rain. I saw that the bare branches of my tree were filled with keening women wrapped in black shawls. They had settled on the bushes and on the barbed wire fence, and in my aunt's voice they were speaking to me: "Remember, be sure to do what I deserve, as I asked you to.... Do not disgrace my dead body.... No lipstick, no powder.... Examine my shroud, make sure it's not full of mites, God forbid.... Do not forget the Willett Street rabbis. I've made my donations so they will say Kaddish and study Mishnah in my name. Remember! Remember!"

"I remember," I answered into the pillow.

I pulled the covers over my head, but the wailing women in the March wind kept up their lament. They commanded me to read and understand the wind-blown pages of my aunt's life. Eyes shut, I gazed upon the narrow lane where she was born and grew up. Here she is as a little girl, playing with the boys who study at her father's school. And now she's a grown woman, sitting at the machine, sewing bridal garments for other women's weddings. She sews and sews, until white begins to show in her jet-black braids. Then she bows to her father's wishes and marries a widower with grown children. When her father dies, her husband takes over the school and his children leave for America. My aunt's mother moves in with her older daughter, my own mother. Just before the Second World War, my aunt and her husband arrive in New York.

Her husband didn't last long. The strange new country sapped his will to live, and he fell ill and soon died. After his death, his children washed their hands of her. Alone in a strange world, without a relative or a protector, her old home in ruins, my aunt drifted from place to place, hungry, not knowing where to turn, until someone suggested she clean houses for a living.

To ward off the humiliations of the outside world, my aunt took refuge in the secret passages of her own being. There she found a strength that guided her and motivated her to go on with her life. With every punishment in this world of lies and falsehoods, she attained a higher moral standing in the world of truth beyond the grave. She looked forward to the just and agreeable world to come, knowing that there she would be rewarded. Every moment of every day, every day of the year, she prepared herself for the journey to the other world. Mondays and Thursdays, in accordance with the old custom, she fasted half the day.

When we arrived in America, we tracked down my aunt on Powell Street in Brownsville. She was living in a dark cubicle; the landlady kept the toilet locked. That very day, we moved her in with us on Ocean Avenue. We gave her a room with a window overlooking Prospect Park. My aunt, who was barely sixty years old, was already well along on the road to the other world. She didn't meddle in the running of the household. She cooked for herself in her room, kept kosher, prayed in the morning and in the evening. Forever bent over her holy books, she rarely lifted her eyes to see what was happening here on God's earth.

As evening fell, when her room began to grow dark and the shadows pressed in from every corner, after she had finished eating and recited the blessing after the meal, made up her bed and placed a bowl of water on the night table for the next morning's ritual hand washing — then my aunt would emerge from her room to tell the children a story.

She'd recount the tale of the little old lady who had lots and lots of children — dark, charming little girls and boys — Jewish children who spoke Yiddish, studied Torah, and feared God.

Once, when the little old lady had to go into the forest to gather kindling, she warned the children to be good and say their prayers before bed so that no evil would befall them.

The children did as they were told. They said their prayers and went to sleep.

Then a brown bear came running, not from the forest but from far away, from the great cities of the civilized world. And this bear gobbled up all the children. But it so happened that the youngest, the weakest and finest of them all, little Yisrolik, was spared.

Yisrolik was a stargazer. The distant stars called to him. He conducted nighttime vigils high up in the mountains or deep in the valleys. There he read the signs of the Zodiac as they wandered across the heavens. But when Yisrolik came home and saw the disaster that had occurred, he took up his spyglass and set off for the land of his ancestors.

On Friday nights, with the beginning of the Sabbath, my aunt came to life. A special spirit shone from her gray eyes and her face became smooth and unwrinkled. She bought meat from the kosher butcher who adhered to the strictest standards, stewed carrots and baked a sweet kugel. She took her best dress out of the closet and laid it on the bed, next to the white silk kerchief with golden fringes that she wore to bless the candles.

My aunt had brought this kerchief with her from Poland. It was the only memento she had from her mother, and she had decided to wear it when the time came to stand before the Lord of the Universe. She had also sewn for herself a shroud with long sleeves and a high, ruffled collar, as befitted a pious woman.

With every passing day, my aunt became more devout, more observant, withdrawing all the more from the material world.

"Why don't you go to the park now and then?" I would ask. "Fill your lungs with a little fresh air, chat with the other women...."

"I don't have time, my child," she'd say. "I still have so much to do
... and for me the sun is already beginning to set."

When our family expanded and the apartment on Ocean Avenue
became too crowded, we decided to buy a house on Long Island.
Unexpectedly, my aunt refused to come with us. She wasn't familiar
with the neighborhood — maybe it had no synagogue. Now, at her
advanced age, she wasn't about to live among gentiles — not even
Jewish gentiles.

My aunt was seventy years old when she went into the old age
home. She turned over everything she owned and began to save again.
Every penny I gave her she put away — to support the rabbis, the
scholars, long, long after her death. She wouldn't allow herself a piece
of fruit or a dress. Everything went into the little purse that hung
around her neck like an amulet.

My aunt had no children of her own. No matter how much I did
for her, she always felt that children of her own would have done better: a son would have said Kaddish, a daughter would have donated
to charity to save her soul from disgrace in the other world. The way
things were, the entire burden fell on her shoulders.

Every Sunday, I visited my aunt in the old age home. She was
busy there, perhaps reciting a chapter of the Psalms for a sick person
or penning a letter for a poor soul who didn't know how to write.
As time went by, I noticed some odd remarks creeping into her
speech.

"You see that woman over there? She's the youngest daughter of
our kosher slaughterer — you remember her from back home. There
she was a big shot, but here she's a sad case, poor thing. She's ashamed
to look me in the eye. She wants me to think she's from Warsaw —
imagine! Well, if it makes her feel good, I don't mind. . . ."

This wasn't the only such example. In fact, my aunt peopled the
home with characters from the Old Country. The rope-maker from

her town had turned up here and was overseeing the kosher kitchen. The tenant farmer's son had become the house doctor. The cantor was the same one who used to lead the prayers in the big synagogue. The doctor assured me her confusion was caused by hardening of the arteries, but I had my own interpretation. My aunt was running away from the old age home, escaping back to the shtetl. She was going home, back to her youth, back to her roots. Step by step, as if descending a ladder, she was returning to her beginnings, her own Genesis.

One Sunday evening, she called me by the name of her sister, my mother.

"Pesenyu," she said, "I have something to tell you, but remember, don't tell a soul." She moved her chair closer to mine. Her eyes sparkled, and her white hair peeked out from under her kerchief like the unruly curls of a young girl.

"Listen to this," she said. "Motele Shoyber has turned up again. How he figured out where I live, I have no idea. Please, Pesenyu, don't breathe a word to Papa."

She looked me in the eye, then smiled as if to someone behind me. I turned aside, not wanting her to see that I knew she was rambling.

"He's walking back and forth in front of the window," she said, "just like in the good old days. I plead with him — 'How can this be, Motele, you have a wife and children, what do you want with me?'

"'You're my one true love,' he answers — 'it was ordained in heaven.'

"Last night I had just finished saying the prayer for the end of the Sabbath. The lights hadn't yet been turned on. All of a sudden I hear someone tapping at the window — not banging, God forbid, but gently, pleadingly. I look out — it's Motl.

"'What are you doing here in all this rain?' I ask.

"'Open up, Rokhele,' he begs me. He flashes a look with his Gypsy eyes. I go hot and cold. I'm scared to death — Papa could walk in at any moment. But Motl won't give up.

"'Rokhele, darling, open the window, I'm dying for you!' His red-hot eyes burn holes in the windowpane. I cover my face. I don't want to look at him. I don't want to see the net he's spreading for me. I grab the holy book lying on the table. All the virtues of my mother and father come to my aid. And even though I don't turn around again, I can tell he's still there — so sad, so forlorn."

My aunt cried, and I cried along with her.

All summer she fantasized about Motele. By the beginning of autumn, she was slipping rapidly. Around Hanukkah, she had become a little girl . . . running around barefoot, washing her mother's noodle-board in the river . . . setting down the noodle-board in the water and swimming away with the current.

Her mind didn't always wander. These excursions into the past took place mostly in the evening, when she would lay aside her prayer book and sit in her room with only the walls for company. She seldom complained about her fate and even stopped envying the women who had children of their own.

"God works in mysterious ways," she would say. "We human beings with our limited understanding cannot comprehend God's ways."

I lay in bed thinking about our limited understanding. The March wind had blustered away somewhere, taking with it the keening women who spoke to me in my aunt's voice. I also thought about the philosopher who said that a little knowledge is a dangerous thing. Indeed, I knew a little. Lately, when she'd begun calling me Mama, I knew that her end was near. I'd even asked the secretary to call me promptly at the slightest change in her condition.

Well, they had let me know after it was too late, and now God's mysterious ways were enough to make me lose my mind.

Again and again I imagined her despair. She'd been counting on my last visit. She'd had so much to say, so much she wanted to hear. I imagined how she'd wrestled with Death, mounted her resistance, waited and hoped that at any moment the door would open and I would arrive. Until five in the evening she held off the Angel of Death. When night fell, her thoughts became muddled as usual, her wits distracted. Then, only then, was she defeated.

If only they had called me in time, I could have been standing at her death bed, perhaps wearing the white wings of the Angel Gabriel. I would have opened the gates to the Garden of Eden for her. With all due ceremony, I would have shown her to the seat she so richly deserved, where the patriarchs and matriarchs and all righteous men and women sing the Song of Praise before the Throne of God.

At daybreak I arose, ironed the garment she'd sewn for herself, wrapped it in tissue paper, and set off for the funeral. In the lobby, the women fell upon me: "How could you have been so cold-hearted? Her wailing could have moved a stone, but you chose not to respond. They said in the office that they'd called you — the poor woman was waiting for you until the moment her soul departed."

I followed a man who led me down to the basement to identify my aunt's body. She was lying in an open coffin, wrapped in cheap linen basted together with big stitches.

Frozen with fear, I stood and looked at her. I had to do it — I had to — the demand took hold with iron claws. I looked at my escort. "Get out!" I said in a voice that allowed no opposition. He stared at me, startled, but said nothing.

When he had gone, I unwrapped the shroud with its ruffled collar and frilly sleeves. I pulled it over her thin frame, all the way from her feet to her blue lips. I covered her head with the special burial cap, and over the cap I placed her mother's white silk kerchief edged with golden fringe. I pulled the kerchief over her closed eyes. Only her long, pointy nose poked out at me.

Bracing myself against fear, against death, against my own feelings, I touched my lips to the silk kerchief, and it seemed to me that with this gesture I freed the imprisoned soul, which then rose, fluttering softly, and wafted away to the exalted place for which it was destined, leaving behind the body as a gift for Mother Earth.

IMAGES ON A BLANK CANVAS

Through the sun-drenched streets of Tel Aviv I follow the coffin carrying my girlhood friend Zosye to her eternal rest. Inside my head, black crows caw loudly around the dead body, blocking the streets and the passersby and the hearse at the head of the procession. Their din prevents me from gaining access to the ways and byways that led Zosye into prostitution.

It is my first visit to Israel. Intending to go to Eilat, I had already checked out of my room in Tel Aviv and packed my toothbrush when the head of our immigrant society called to invite me to the funeral. I have long since learned to skip over the place where my cradle once stood and instead to seek my origins in the stony strata of history — to search for the living source under the sands of the Negev, shadowed by time, to sail through the gates of the desert and steer my ship along its fated course.

I have placed a film of artificial frost over the small window that looks back into my past. There, white trees and dead roses are always in bloom, not as a memorial, but as a reminder that the layer of ice is an illusion, nothing but the thinnest skin stretched over black depths where snakes and scorpions feed on the remains of their unburied victims.

Whenever I encounter someone who has escaped from the abyss, I look at him with terror, expecting to discover something that disturbs my sense of how things are.

As I ride along in the car, my eye follows the carriage carrying Zosye's martyred bones. I seem to hear the letters "s" and "z" dangerously sharp in her Polish name. Zosye, Zoshke, the bookkeeper's pampered daughter, is riding her bicycle, her windblown hair as blond as the furniture in her father's parlor. When Zosye laughs, the rows of trees lining the road respond with an emphatic "yes!"

Many girls in our small town spoke Polish, but Zosye's Polish had deep roots. Absorbed with the milk of her gentile wet nurse, it was a mark of her dual identity.

I leaf through the pages fluttering in my mind. The black crows retreat into the background. The open path ahead leads to the town where I grew up. I follow the town princess to the shadowy corners of the world, and to the sea, to the blue shores of the Mediterranean into which she threw herself. I don't see her the way she looks now. Sealed in the coffin, she is safe from curious eyes. She is no longer for sale, neither to earn money nor out of despair. Against her will she arrived in this world, and against her will she has departed.

Three other people are sharing the car with me. They, too, are shuffling through pages — pages marked with judgments. "She was a streetwalker who lived with an Arab." They exchange information they have observed with their own eyes. I am trying to see the invisible. I don't trust the eye that relies on facts. Half-truths can mislead, divert the guilt from murderer to murdered. The corpse is silent, and the murderer, protected by the privileged status accorded him as a cit-

izen, a father, and perhaps by now a grandfather, sips his beer in peace
and grows fatter by the day.

"Why didn't she adapt to the new way of life? Why didn't she
become a productive member of society like other immigrants?"

I don't answer these questions. The truth is concealed beneath
bloody bandages; the painful wound may not be touched. It is clear
that a single standard does not fit all. I believe no suicide is an accident.
Every hour, every moment, the suicide holds the blade over her throat.
Zosye committed her first suicide — her initial, spiritual suicide —
in Felix's attic. The physical one came gradually, step by step.

I meander along the victim's own paths. I know who murdered
her. In exchange for a piece of bread and a slice of ham, he sated
himself on her blooming, sun-ripened white body. Perhaps she committed suicide even earlier. Perhaps her life ended on the wild
autumn night when Felix arrived like a prince on a white horse,
bearing a loaf of bread and a peasant skirt, blouse, and kerchief. Zosye
donned the clothes and kissed her mother's wet face, black as that
autumn night. . . . She kissed the dog that lay by the door without
understanding that the house he was guarding had become a prison.
She kissed her father's body, which had lain abandoned in the marketplace after he was shot. She kissed the piano and the garden that
surrounded the house. Everything, everything she gathered up inside
her, hiding it like a ransom in the cellars of her being.

Behind Felix's barn, downhill from the path, stood a pond bordered
by linden trees. Beneath its slimy green surface, fish were spawning.
On sunny days Zosye could see them swimming in the water. She
could see the black rings on the green-mirrored surface. Through the
narrow crevices in the attic, these rings became the only outlet for
her famished gaze. Looking down, she would imagine the ring she'd
create when she threw herself into the water. Buried deep in the hay,
she had time to mourn her own death and to attend her own funeral.

Now, on the way to her funeral, I want to tell her that I see with her eyes, feel with her senses. I picture perspiring beds. I caress bodies with her fingers. I do it in the spirit of the girl I once knew, searching for a sign of today in the buried world of yesterday. In that light, or more aptly put, in those shadows, I seek to glimpse the why and the wherefore. In my mind I lower myself into the abyss, following the overgrown footpath to long-ago.

Sometimes in those days, after I'd brought my father his coffee in the butcher shop, I would stop at Zosye's exquisite garden on my way home. Standing on tiptoe, I'd peer over the fence and marvel at the golden lilies that grew around her house. I would bemoan all that could have been but never was. If my grandfather hadn't been so stubborn, if he'd yielded to the demands of Zosye's father's parents and provided them with the dowry they asked for, then I, not she, would have been the bookkeeper's daughter, playing the piano and preparing to travel all the way to Lemberg for my studies. But my pious grandfather was loath to go against his deeply-held ethical beliefs by making a promise he knew he could not keep, and so the bookkeeper and my mother had parted forever. He married a rich man's daughter, and my mother married a butcher boy.

I used to stand at the fence and imagine how it would have been, if only. . . .

Today, as a tourist from Paris, I accompany the bookkeeper's daughter to her eternal rest and remember how gladly I would have relinquished all my worldly ambitions to study in Lemberg.

Through the skylight of my Parisian garret I used to look up at the tiny rectangle of heaven that fortune had allotted me and conjure up Zosye's lush, slumbering garden. How I cursed the fate that had stranded me in Paris on my way to Israel!

Zosye did not want to go to Israel, nor did she need to. For her, the vine was abloom with all the brilliant hues of the bejeweled peacock that resides in the dreams of every young woman.

How could she have known, as she played the piano, that the civilization of those magical notes was even then writing her people's death sentence? How could she have known that form and harmony were but the seductive song of the Lorelei, the façade behind which the cannibal sharpened his crooked teeth? Protected and sheltered like the golden lilies in her father's garden, Zosye could not see those teeth. With the natural power that is the birthright of every living thing, she glowed in the light of the sun. Endowed with all the attributes she needed to thrive and grow, Zosye was primed to scatter her own seeds across God's willing earth.

The pages I turn are blank, as unreadable as the image in a shattered mirror. It occurs to me that the earth to which Zosye is now returning holds the remains of another prostitute, the biblical Tamar, who sat down at the crossroads where fortunes were decided and seduced men with her charms. I search for a spark of Tamar's desire in the image of Zosye that is anchored deep in my memory. I search for the lust of a whore in her dimples and her rosy, Polish-speaking lips that surely didn't even know the meaning of the word "prostitute." I look into her eyes, the reflection of her soul. Her character, unripe, uprooted, is borne by the wind to the four corners of the world. I search for the legacy of modesty passed down through the generations. I search for the set path of her father, and before me another form rises up: her Uncle Shloyme, the Russian. I don't force this figure to take shape — I let it grow on its own. I relive the terror that his death caused me, which penetrated my dreams long after I'd left my town behind. His imposing figure rises out of the mist: gray eyes, bushy black eyebrows, broad shoulders, erect and proud. From his mouth I heard for the first time that "all is vanity." When Shloyme spoke, every word burned, a reflection of the grief and rage that gradually devoured him. At the time I imagined he looked the way Job did when he sat down in dust and ashes, despising himself. "What is the difference between man and beast," Shloyme asked, "if even a rabbi will paw at his wife's tits?"

These particular words, expressed at our home one Sabbath afternoon, provoked a radical shift in my thinking. I too began to ask questions that led me off the beaten path. When Shloyme the Russian lay on his death bed, he wanted only one thing: that God should grant him sufficient strength to get out of bed, set the house on fire, and be burned with all his worldly possessions on God's eternal sacrificial altar. And, in fact, this is what he did. People said that years earlier he had been banished from the Jewish community for reading the heretic Spinoza and for walking too far outside the town limits on the Sabbath, in violation of Jewish law.

Did Zosye, too, search for a path to God through alien gardens? Did the tragic worm that consumed Shloyme the Russian make itself at home in her soul and force her to leave the main road and set off on another? Did it force her to walk beyond the Pale and excommunicate herself?

Shloyme the Russian had a legitimate claim against his Creator. His barren wife turned away from the Almighty before he did. She became devoted to black magic, ghosts and spirits, and witches who fed her wild herbs and swindled away a fortune with promises that help would come her way if she followed their directions. And so Shorke the Russian, Shloyme's wife, did as instructed. She strung around her neck the claws of a crow and placed the hairs of a she-panther in her bosom. At midnight she bathed in the milk of a pregnant cow and outlined her navel with the blood of a bull. Her hair unkempt, eyes painted with soot, cheeks rouged with chicory paper, Shorke approached her husband to be fertilized.

In the car all is quiet. I look out onto the winding streets of Jaffa. The sky is a pure, light blue, without a cloud to anchor the mind. The hearse carrying the corpse continues ahead. Parallels multiply; characters who have no obvious connection to one another become entangled like roots under the earth. They worm their way into the core of Zosye's being. They help me to construct a woman from the child of long ago.

I see the woman in Felix's attic. She is speaking to God, pleading with Him to spare her mother and her little sister. She pleads until there is nothing left to plead for. The city has been destroyed. The past is no more. Perhaps it never was? The abyss she is looking into has lost all familiar markers. No signs of yesterday, no indications of tomorrow. The forest in its innocence is in full flower. Fish multiply in the pond. Cicadas call to one another; male and female come together in the deep grasses of the meadow. Zosye knows she is pregnant. The cow in its stall is pregnant, too. Both are silent. The cow chews its cud and ruminates. Zosye picks up a stalk of straw and does the same. She thinks mostly about eating. Not about the wild strawberries with sweet cream that her mother used to serve, but about bread with salt, perhaps with a clove of garlic.

The chickens in the courtyard peck at their grain and carry on with their squabbles. They have no idea that man has confined them in a ghetto for his own gain, that cold, cynical human calculation has lodged them in a comfortable death camp. Whenever he feels like it, he'll grab a cleaver and chop off the white head of a hen, whistling all the while. Zosye is not afraid of death. She accepts Felix's favors like the cicadas in the grass. She doesn't tell him about the pregnancy.

Felix has a wife and children. He keeps Zosye in his mother's attic, holding his mother responsible for her safety. Felix's mother is well aware of her son's desires and knows that he means what he says. She makes sure not to let the Jewess out of the attic. She hides Zosye's food in the bucket of oats for the cow. Felix's mother is talkative. She prattles on at length about how the Germans have shot all the Jews, stacked the corpses like timber, doused them with kerosene and set them ablaze. She doesn't conceal her satisfaction. She hates the Germans, but their savage treatment of the Jews is pleasing to her. "It's high time we were rid of them," she says.

Zosye doesn't tell Felix about his mother's chatter. She has long since stopped complaining, either to God or to people. She lies in the attic and listens as the front draws closer every day. The stable trembles with the heavy shelling that rolls like spring thunder. Zosye does not wait for tomorrow or hold onto today. Now that liberation is near, she wants only to sleep. In her dreams she has a past. She has a father, a mother, a clearly demarcated path, a straight line between two mountains of snow. She glides on ice skates; diamonds sparkle in the sun. Overwhelmed with bliss, she closes her eyes just for a moment — then loses her way in a fierce blizzard.

Zosye sleeps. She wants to gorge on the dream until she chokes. But when the liberator bangs on the door, she can't find the strength to get up and open it. Instead, she lies there, listening to the cells dividing in her bloodstream. She takes her pulse and counts her heartbeats. She descends deeper and deeper into the black shafts of consciousness. Inch by inch Zosye draws back into herself. The footsteps of the liberator echo rhythmically on the road. She has no road. Her paths are overgrown with grass. She digs into the earth, under the weeds, touches the root with its suicidal poison — then gets up and climbs out of the attic. She pauses next to the cow. For a long time they stare at each other in mute understanding.

Slowly and carefully, Zosye walks down the hill between newly planted garden beds. She goes to the pond covered with green slime, closes her eyes, and throws herself in.

Zosye opens her eyes in the hospital. A bit of congealed blood trembles in a glass by the side of her bed. "A four-month-old soul," says the nurse. "Everything inside you was rotten. It all had to be removed."

Zosye smiles and says nothing. She asks no questions; she has no wish to know. Perhaps she thinks about her aunt, the barren Shorke? The truth is she is utterly indifferent. She lies in bed until she's ordered to leave. Along with other wind-blown wanderers, she roams from camp to camp. But even here she's alone. Zosye tries to go with the current. But the severed branches, leaves, and stones carried by the flow get in her way, piling their dead weight on her young shoulders. They paralyze her will, cutting her off from the stream of history and pulling her down into the abyss.

Sometimes, when Felix was tormenting her, the tears would come like a benign rain. He was the rod of punishment whose blows she endured for the sin of abandoning her mother and sister to their deaths. Each bite of bread she paid for with self-torment and self-hatred. The same feeling of guilt followed her to Israel.

At war with herself and with a reality to which she could not adjust, Zosye searched for meaning and found it in self-abasement. The deeper she sank into the swamp, the more entitled she felt to walk on God's earth.

Zosye lay on the bottom and allowed herself to waste away. Like the Greek god Prometheus, bound to a rock, his insides gouged by an eagle, she stood with her belly exposed to the predatory birds of the world. And when the birds of prey had nothing left to peck at, she went to the sea, just as she had once gone to the pond, and threw herself in.

Enveloped in silence, I sit alone in the car. I, too, am avoiding reality. In the distance her grave is being covered. A man with a long beard and a broad-brimmed hat is reciting a prayer. I see that he's hurrying. Soon he'll recite the same prayer at another grave. I don't need to hear what he's saying. Instead I listen to the prayer that trembles inside me, a prayer that can never be repeated. It is a prayer without words, a prayer buried deep in the collective consciousness of my people. The man with the beard rushes on. Somewhere another corpse awaits him. The prayer I recite has no end. It seethes and bubbles like a chemical brew on the brink of existing. In the mixture I look for the symbol that Zosye lost. I must find it and clean off the mud, the impurity, the shame.

I know I will return, perhaps tomorrow, perhaps a year from now. Using the new-found symbol, I will erect a tombstone, a blank stone without words. The passerby who stops will have to create Zosye's image from what is not stated. He'll stand before the stone like a master before a blank canvas. Among all the images that leap into his mind, he will need to see first of all that Zosye is the crow that pecks at my conscience.

Neighbors over the Fence

Every time Betty looks up from her typewriter, Mrs. Zagretti's whitewashed stoop catches her eye. She knows that the widow will open her front door at exactly 9:00 a.m. Without even looking, she can see the woman's wintry face shrouded in its black shawl. The gulls lying in wait on nearby rooftops have no need of a clock either. As soon as they finish their first breakfast at sea, they show up at Mrs. Zagretti's for dessert — tasty bread crumbs dipped in fat and salted just so, as if she knows exactly how they like it.

The moment the door opens, the birds attack, flapping raucously over the fence to land on her shoulders. Bowl in hand, Mrs. Zagretti tosses bits of bread over the railing. The clever gulls catch the food in midair. Once they've gobbled up the last morsels, she goes back into the house. The birds linger on surrounding roofs to wait for more, but when the miracle fails to occur, they fly back out to sea, where the bowl of food is never empty.

Betty doesn't wear a watch. She likes to rely on the widow.

At about ten o'clock, a taxi arrives to transport Mrs. Zagretti to her son's grocery store. At three in the afternoon, she returns home laden with groceries and stale bread for the insatiable birds.

When Betty is busy with a literary text, she loses track of time. Only when Mrs. Zagretti's taxi appears does she realize she must put away her work before the children come home from school.

Betty works at the machine only in winter. In summer she devotes herself to the children. Also, in hot weather, friends she hasn't heard from all winter call on the telephone. They come for a swim in the sea and stay for supper, leaving behind wet towels and a carpet full of sand.

Betty's friendship with the widow began over the fence. The two of them sought to display their horticultural know-how, each on her own turf. Mrs. Zagretti won the contest. Not only did she have a green thumb — all ten fingers yielded a plentiful crop. She was privy to the secrets of the green world, knew what the plants wanted and lovingly fulfilled their every need. She showed her Jewish neighbor which ones needed full sun, which could manage with less. The two exchanged tomato seedlings, cucumbers, zucchini, a variety of flowers.

"Life, my dear, is a garden full of all kinds of plants," Mrs. Zagretti said. "People, too, are plants that must be cultivated if they are to reach their highest potential."

In the summer, Mrs. Zagretti spent all day in her garden. She cared for every plant as if it were a living creature, caressing each with her hands, her eyes, and, it seemed to Betty, her heart.

The pride of her garden was the fig tree, which had been imported from Italy. During the winter, the tree was wrapped from top to toe in a black cloth. In April, when all danger of frost had passed, Mrs. Zagretti uncovered the tree as reverently as one would unwrap the mummy of an ancient pharaoh. The delivery of the tree into the hands of the spring sun always took place on a Sunday, before mass. Then, usually on Good Friday, the whole family — her son and daughter-in-law, the daughter-in-law's parents, and their children — would take part in a ceremony, dancing around the tree as if it were a pagan god.

With a little sun, a little rain, and a little organic fertilizer, the tree would begin to sprout. Red buds appeared among the branches. They grew fuller every day, until, to Mrs. Zagretti's delight, leaves burst open like green spoons in the sunshine. Every morning and evening she watered the tree, counting the blossoms and later the fruits. She spoke to the tree in Italian.

At the end of September, when the widow Zagretti harvested her figs, she talked to herself in a melodious voice, perhaps even singing a song as she worked. Over the fence, she presented Betty with a dozen of the green fruits on a plate covered with an embroidered cloth.

"You're the only one who appreciates the fruits of my fig tree," she said. "My own daughter-in-law doesn't deserve them. Anyone who says that figs from a can are as good as the ones from a tree isn't worthy of a real, natural fruit — a fruit grown without chemicals or artificial fertilizer, a fruit as God created it. But what can you expect from an American girl who paints her fingernails and dyes her hair!"

Betty obliged her neighbor. She extolled the figs and assured Mrs. Zagretti that only an Italian tree could have produced such delicious fruit. Her interactions with the widow were unfailingly warm and sincere. She listened to her talk about the same topics over and over: the garden, the economy, her son's grocery store, and the shortcomings of her American daughter-in-law.

One fine winter day when Betty is busy at her typewriter, Mrs. Zagretti knocks at the door. Looking out the window and seeing her on the way, Betty can't believe her eyes. In the three years since she and her family moved into the neighborhood, the widow has never once darkened her doorstep, nor has Betty ever set foot in her house.

The friendship has never crossed over the fence. For the first year, Mrs. Zagretti deliberately ignored the Jewish family. She seemed to have decided not to see Betty's friendly smile or to respond to her greetings. The house had previously belonged to an Italian family, and Mrs. Zagretti was unable to adapt to the change. Not until spring arrived, when the two women began working in the garden, did they forge an unexpected connection, an emotional affinity that bound them like roots intertwined under the fence.

Mrs. Zagretti noticed that contrary to expectations her Jewish neighbor had a natural gift for gardening. It was Betty's ungloved hands that gave her away. Standing on her side of the fence, she was surprised to see Betty scratching at the soil with bare fingers — something her daughter-in-law would never have done. She leaned over the fence and offered her new neighbor half a dozen gladiolus bulbs, along with instructions as to how to plant and tend them, how to dig them up at the end of the summer, how to store them for the next season.

The second spring, Mrs. Zagretti presented Betty with some tomato plants started from seed that were ready to be put into the ground. Every morning the two women greeted each other with a friendly "Good morning," and every evening they wished each other a good night. But they never invited each other into their homes. The garden brought them together, and as the garden blossomed, so did the friendship — but never did it cross their thresholds.

Now, when the widow knocks at the door, Betty greets her with undisguised amazement. She isn't sure whether to invite her in or deal with her in the doorway. Sensing her hesitation, Mrs. Zagretti steps in without ceremony. "Close the door," she says. "No sense letting the heat out."

Mrs. Zagretti removes her coat but not the black shawl covering her head. She sits down and fingers her rosary as if she were seated before the priest in a confession booth rather than in a Jewish home.

Betty flutters around her guest, making coffee and waiting for her to speak.

"Why didn't you go to your son at the store?" she asks. "Is something wrong?"

Mrs. Zagretti stares at her neighbor in surprise. "Ah, you notice everything," she says. "No, I couldn't bring myself to do business on a day like today."

Betty sips her coffee and studies her older neighbor out of the corner of her eye. Mrs. Zagretti has not touched her coffee. Something has definitely happened, Betty decides. Or is today a religious holiday? No, it has to be something personal — the shadow clouding her neighbor's face attests to that. Her nose seems sharper than ever and her cheeks are sunken, with no sign of their summer color. Only the severe black line of her eyebrows hints at her former radiance.

Mrs. Zagretti sits silently, absorbed in herself — until suddenly she stands up and makes a sweeping gesture with her hand. "Too bad your walls are so bare!" she exclaims.

"What do you mean?" Betty asks.

"The people before you had holy pictures on the walls."

"But Jews don't put up religious pictures," Betty says.

"A house without a picture, my mother used to say, is like a heart without a god," Mrs. Zagretti says. "When I pray to God, I need a picture in front of me."

"We Jews carry God in our hearts," Betty says, an edge in her voice.

"I know," says Mrs. Zagretti, "I know you do. I often see you standing by the window. Only people who are close to God have such a look. I understand people, you know — maybe not with my brains but with something I got from my ancestors. I have a feeling you have that something inside you, too, Betty. That's why I find it easier to talk to you than to my daughter-in-law, my son, or even my priest."

"Thank you, Mrs. Zagretti," Betty says. "You're too kind."

The widow doesn't answer. She hurries down the hall to the doorway. Her face lights up with a summery smile as she tightens the shawl around her head and buttons her coat. A hidden hand seems to have erased the wrinkles from her face. She clears her throat and says, "Can you imagine a person feeling close to a fly?"

"To a what?"

"A fly," Mrs. Zagretti says. "A housefly. Do you know what I mean?"

"I think so," Betty answers. "Yes, of course I do."

"You're not laughing at me?"

"No," says Betty. "Why should I laugh? A fly is one of God's creatures, isn't it?"

The widow fingers her beads again. Her smile has disappeared. "You might not think a person and a fly would have anything to do with each other," she says. "The person didn't invite the fly into the house, or make a nest for the fly, or put out food for the fly. And yet . . . do you understand what I'm saying?"

Betty nods.

In the open doorway, Mrs. Zagretti leans against the jamb just the way she leans on the fence. Clearly she feels freer outside. Her words pour out:

"You won't believe how much grief this fly is causing me. I came into the kitchen this morning and there it was, lying like a crumb on the windowsill — dead! What can I tell you? My arms and legs went numb. I felt as if I'd become a widow for the second time."

Betty looks at the floor without speaking. She reaches out and touches the widow's shoulder.

Mrs. Zagretti shakes herself as if awakening from a trance. "How can I put it?" she says. "The fly was a kind of soulmate for me. Whenever I came home it flew to greet me. It followed me from room to room. At night when I got into bed it would circle around the night-light. Around and around and around — it must have been trying to get back to the warm nest where it was born. It wasn't fully grown — it must have hatched in late summer, so that its life was just beginning when all the rest of its species had already died. I could feel the tragedy of being left all alone in the world — all ties severed, friends and relations annihilated without a trace, condemned by fate to live out its one and only life in anguish. . . . "

Betty wants to say that she knows many people who were orphaned and left alone in the world — not because of a mistake in the calendar but because of the calculated, brutal, organized murder of a people.

A wind stirs the bare branches of the trees. Mrs. Zagretti's lips have turned blue with cold.

"Maybe I'll go down to the store after all," she says. "What did my son do to deserve such a foolish mother?"

"Good idea," Betty says. "Go on, Mrs. Zagretti. We'll talk about all this another time."

THE DEBT

She lay face up on the operating table. Her upper body was firmly secured with plastic straps. Her knees were up, her bare legs spread.

She was not thinking of the danger ahead. She'd left all her doubts and self-pity in the sixth-floor garret where they'd first taken root inside her, had abandoned them there like a stack of unsigned poems — odes, perhaps, to the patch of sky that pressed against her tiny skylight. Here on the table she felt calm, suffused with the perverse serenity that comes sometimes when all seems lost. Behind her eyelids, she held onto the summer morning that had settled on the edge of her consciousness, blocking out the reality of what was to come.

It was an ordinary morning. The soft golden fingers of the sun had touched the first story of Sacre Coeur Basilica and were groping through the lush leaves of the chestnut trees toward the statue of the boy, from whose stone member a falling stream was trickling.

The operating room had no windows. The light from neon bulbs hit the ceiling and bounced to the floor. The girl on the table kept her eyes closed. She saw no one. She heard voices coming from another world, a world with which she had no connection whatsoever. They were speaking of someone she did not want to know. She took refuge in the vision of the summer morning, sheltering within it even after the nurse placed the ether mask over her nose.

A voice instructed her to count: *un, deux, trois.* She placed her mouth under the innocent member of the stone boy so that the cold water would spurt out over her face, her whole body: *quatre, cinq, six, sept.*

If this was to be her last breath, it was good that it was happening here, by the statue of the boy, and good that it was early, before the mothers with their baby carriages filled the square.

Standing by her head, the nurse pressed the mask to her face with a tender, womanly touch. Her right hand held the mask; her left stroked the girl's brow. The girl on the table surrendered to the nurse's cool fingers. She herself had always wanted to be a nurse.

"*Respirez, mademoiselle.*" The voice was hypnotic. Twenty-two, twenty-three. The room began to spin. The voices drowned, surfaced, went under again. The waters were black and deep. Rather than foaming like the sea they were still: a stagnant lake of chloroform. She was a stripe of neon light trembling on the surface, pointing in no direction.

She felt hands penetrating her intimate parts, sliding in and out like fish. The calm that had overtaken her was as deep as the water, like a whirlpool revolving around a single thought, a murky thought that did not touch her true self. The drama was taking place behind a curtain. On this side of the scene all was utterly calm.

The voices emerging from the deep did not concern her. They were speaking of someone in whom she had not the slightest interest. They were talking about the girl lying on the table: such a young thing, four months pregnant.

In the recovery room, she recalled these words but did not want to think about them. With her eyes she followed the nurse gliding by with light, graceful steps. The nurse came to her side, wiped her face, removed the basin of vomit, tucked in her covers.

Only then did she notice that she was lying near a window. The shutters were closed, but she could hear rain and see gray strips of daylight. Birds were stirring somewhere nearby. Probably there was a garden, flowers, trees.

Across the room, a woman was vomiting, her face hidden behind a tangle of red locks. A young man with prematurely gray hair bent over her, helping her to settle back on the pillow and spreading out her curls in a fiery circle.

The nurse moved from bed to bed. Her steps were rhythmic; they swaddled thought like ether masks, clouding the moment, keeping reality at bay.

In the next bed, a woman was combing her hair. As she looked into the mirror, she addressed a listener who wasn't there. Could she be talking to me? the girl wondered. She unrolled an endless spool of words about her family, her husband, her children. Her husband was never satisfied, she said. They made love day and night, but it was no longer love; it was a nightmare.

Her words pressed on the girl's spirit like a layer of asphalt. Feeling chilled to the bone, she leaned over the basin and vomited. On the bedside table she spied her watch. He who should be visiting — was he late? Or perhaps not coming at all?

The young man with prematurely gray hair was kissing the red-head's hands. She was still quite young, perhaps fifteen or sixteen. Her face was an interesting mix: a sharply-drawn profile with high cheek-bones and an upturned nose, a low hairline and a small mouth, open and enchanting.

The woman in the next bed was packing her things. This was her fourth time in the hospital. Wrinkles showed through powder on her face. Her neck was layered in fat. She pulled up her stockings over blue-veined legs. Her husband waited by her side, looking not at her but at the redhead.

The girl wondered whether she envied the redhead. Would she, too, like a hand on her brow, a word whispered in her ear? Did she wish he would come?

The redhead was French; the art of love was in her blood. She, on the other hand, was nothing more than an imitation, making a fool of herself by aping others.

If she were to die here, everything would work itself out. Her friend would write to her father and say she had been killed in an accident. Or maybe he wouldn't. He was nothing but a stranger, after all.

The redhead was kissing her lover's palm, covering it with both hands and holding it to her lips.

Where she stood was somewhere in between the redheaded girl and the powdered lady. Except that she was not standing — she was flying, her aircraft steered by erotic winds. Would she come back to earth and land safely on both feet?

Her little room on the sixth floor would no doubt be growing dark by now, the gray patch of sky gradually disappearing from view. She would lie in her bed watching the gray walls darken and close in. She would count the footsteps on the stairs. Would anyone stop at her door?

Do I want him to come? What do I have to say to him? What do I want to hear? A virgin, four months pregnant. . . . No, she would not tell him, would not even consider it. He'd paid for his pleasure. The account was settled, paid in full.

How quickly it had happened, she thought. The very same week she'd lost her job, her father's letter had arrived with the news that he was sick, needed an operation, and had no money. She owed her father a debt. He had sold his part of the inheritance to send her to Paris. In truth, he was about to remarry and wanted to be rid of his grown daughter. For her part, she wanted to be as far away as possible from the new couple.

The letter was like a lock that slammed the shackles around her, psychological shackles from which she could not free herself — or from which, perhaps, she did not wish to be freed.

"I need a loan," she told the man — older, married, wealthy — whose admiration for her was unbounded. The idea had entered her head unexpectedly; the words emerged from her mouth as if spoken not by her but by someone with the worldview of a Claudette or a Simone.

"How much?" he asked.

"Five thousand francs."

"That's all?"

"Yes," she said, "to pay for my father's operation."

"You are a child," he said. "It's not enough." As he spoke, he was locking the door, turning off the light. She did not see his face. She heard his voice, hot, insistent, hoarse. She thought of her father. Or maybe she did not think at all. She closed her eyes. How quickly it all happened. A double operation, father's and daughter's . . . and Mother lying in her grave, doubly dishonored.

One thought followed another, like links in a chain. She dozed, then woke. A new patient had been moved into the next bed and a nurse was preparing her for the operation. The redhead with the flawless profile, like Ingres's "Odalisque," was filing her nails. She smiled at the empty chair where her lover had been sitting.

A new day pushed at the tightly closed shutters. Only now did she feel the pain in her belly — a sharp pain, as if a thousand dogs were gnawing at her insides. Her body was on fire, but she refused a sleeping pill.

"Can I bring you a lemonade?" the nurse asked, concerned. "Coffee or tea?"

No, she wanted nothing. She wanted to feel the pain down to her bones. She wanted to burn off the scar tissue, to peel off the mask, to know herself.

In the green meadow of her youth she sees the girl playing with pieces of broken glass. She finds a miraculous splinter that reveals a wondrous world of red and green and blue. Strings of beads, green pearls. The nettles sparkle like seven suns and the stones in the road are golden coins.

The blond peasant boy from across the river sticks out his foot to trip her and snatches away the magic shard. The girl cries. The girl inside her is still crying, has never stopped. The peasant boy has smashed the magic glass, stomped it to pieces.

"Is it still possible for me to become a nurse?" she asked faintly.

"Of course it is," the nurse answered. "Two years of study and this vomit basin will be yours. With all the trimmings."

She turned to face the wall. The girl in the green meadow of long ago dries her eyes. She looked off into the distance, lost in thought, and fell asleep.

MY FRIEND BEN

Lying under my apple tree, I make a conscious effort to detach myself from the outside world. Eyes closed, I attempt to follow the teachings of Zen Buddhism and rise above the stifling heat, the children's racket, and the airplanes swooping overhead like birds of prey. It's the middle of July. Apollo 11 has landed safely on the moon, a great human achievement that leaves a strange taste in my mouth, a taste I can neither swallow nor spit out.

Needless to say, I feel proud that the human ego has managed to sever the umbilical cord with Mother Earth and go in search of destinies that have slumbered in mankind's imagination since the six days of creation. My heart pounded as I watched the astronauts leave their earthly footprints on a heavenly body that until now had been touched only by the sighs of lovers.

Yet even as I rejoiced in their achievement, a part of me also hoped that some extraordinary force would fend off the terrestrial incursion. I wasn't expecting a metaphysical revolution led by gods or people or even supermen — by now we know all too well what supermen can do. No, I dreamed of something totally unforeseen, something that would liberate me from spiritual stagnation and provide wings for a visionary flight.

I lie with my face to the ground. The heat intensifies. Above the thick layer of industrial pollution, the sun shuffles along indifferently, apathetically, as if it wants nothing to do with the earth. I, too, endeavor to cast off my worldly yoke, to lay down the burden of the daily responsibilities that suck the life out of me. I search for a pathway to a realm beyond the self, beyond the limits of the individual, an exalted sphere where nothing is personal, nothing happens, nothing changes, nothing is good or bad — where time in its indifference consumes murdered and murderer alike, generation after generation.

I lie without moving. Behind my closed eyelids I focus on a single point that will lead me to absolute calm. As if on skates, I glide into a smooth and endless place, deeper and deeper into the viscera of creation, where gravity will dissolve and I will float into eternity, free of feelings, like a mote in the eye of a hurricane.

But to reach the eye of the hurricane, I must traverse the fiery space in between. I must swim across the river of forgiveness, across the black mountains and the green valleys, into the shadowy depths of antiquity, to the roots of human passion. I must forget that my son, who's serving in the Marines, is about to land on the shores of Vietnam. I must stop worrying about my daughter, who has dropped out of college and become a kind of pseudo-primitive, as is fashionable in her generation. She doesn't want an education that will only compound the world's problems. She wants no part in polluting the world. She wants to return to nature and live the way people used to live, not as subjugator or corruptor but at one with the natural world. She wants to repair the wrongs committed by an egocentric civilization, to purify the air for all people, the forests for animals, the waters for fish. She wants to do her part for the miracle of life, not death. She feels an obligation toward every form of life, without exception.

Where she comes by such notions I have no idea. She never looks at a book and avoids television and newspapers. Night and day, all she does is listen to music.

No matter how I try to convince myself that nothing is troubling me, I'm aware of the mosquitoes and the oppressive heat and the strumming of a guitar somewhere nearby. The false notes grate mercilessly on my nerves.

I see the earth rising up to meet the moon, and at the same time I see how the moon in the jungle of Vietnam illuminates the faces of the young who have been shot and wounded. The more I try to concentrate, to escape into myself, the more my thoughts spread out, grasping blindly like fantastical fins at the faces that swim by, some with Asian eyes, some with Western eyes, eyes burning with murderous passion and eyes innocent and calm. From these eyes I absorb the bittersweet taste of conflict, and in them I search for answers.

Zen Buddhism fades away and I return to the stream of ordinary life. Human contradictions fascinate me once again, drawing me as if with a cosmic force. Perhaps a pebble from the moon will cause something new to happen.

I remove my hands from my eyes and allow myself to be carried by the flow of the moment, feeling the twists and turns, the unexpected joys and sorrows of becoming.

Often I share such contemplations with my friend Ben Feder. I throw out ideas and see how he responds. He arrives at my house brimming with the latest articles from the *Times*. He quotes famous people and modestly adds his own commentary.

"This flying to the moon," he says, "reminds me of the adventurous ant who climbs to the roof. She's always believed that the house where she was born and raised was the center of the universe. But when she gets to the roof and sees how many houses there are, big ones and little ones, stretching all the way to the horizon, she's so terrified she goes crazy."

"You've seen a crazy ant?"

Ben takes my hand in his. "I know you could tell it better," he says.

Ben is a good listener. Even when he's down in the dumps, his face displays a sincere interest. He feels he owes the other person a compliment or a smile, and if that person, man or woman, is pleased, he's even more pleased. For him, such gestures are part of the cost of doing business in the game of he-and-she.

My daughter's father will not pay such fees. He offers cash for everything, and if life denies him the payback he expects, he objects with oaths and curses. He claims our daughter is unconsciously living out my own fantasies, crackpot theories she absorbed with her mother's milk.

I tell him that the astronauts themselves are living out someone else's fantasy, that every real-world experience was once a fantasy, a seed carried on the wings of the wind. There's no such thing as starting from scratch, I say. Our lives have been connected, one to the next, ever since a certain romantic gene seduced a sunray and figured out how to be fruitful and multiply. Since that fateful day, all of us have been traveling on the path set by that gene, even if we have no idea where the path is leading.

My daughter's father has neither time nor patience for such "intellectual" sermonizing. Ben Feder has both time and patience. Without a wife or children, he lives with his cat and dog and earns a living giving piano lessons. In fact, that's how I came to know him. My daughter is no longer interested, but Ben continues to stop by. He comes in the morning, when I tend to be alone. While I make breakfast, he sits down at the piano. He begins with Chopin and Beethoven, and as the aroma of coffee fills the house he moves on to the "Malagueña" from the sublime *Suite Andalucia.*

I don't know whether he can tell how deeply the music affects me. Sound merges with sound, spiraling into a storm of emotions. The music ferments, overflowing into my bloodstream, and I absorb it into my being. . . .

Inside her solitary cell, the Persona forgets her chains and rises on fantasy-wings. Clad in a tunic threaded with gold, she dances wantonly before an ethereal vision that swells, takes form, and becomes flesh and blood, his narrow hips swaying before her in velvet and silk. Limbs outstretched, he dances with menacing drama. The music froths and foams. Snorting bulls thunder into the arena. The Persona steps back. Her crimson tunic becomes a fiery cape. The toreador flings open the cape to reveal a bloody sword. The crowd cheers, intoxicated with blood. . . . I open my eyes and the magic spell fades away.

We sit at the table drinking coffee. Ben is as unsettled as I am. On occasion he manages to embrace me. He is neither too forward nor too shy. He just stands like a beggar on my doorstep and accepts whatever alms I slip through the slot.

I offer cheese and sour cream with red strawberries. Ben wipes his brow. The skin around his eyes is dry, with deeply incised grooves, like earth without rain. His lips are cold, as if he keeps them in the icebox. I don't want to hurt him. I laugh and talk, ask after his dog and cat. My interest in his life warms him. The fire in his green eyes, which smolders like the eternal flame in the synagogue, comes blazing forth. As his face comes alive, he grows animated and bold. He pushes his cup away and takes my hand.

"We're not the only ones with problems," he says. "Animals have problems, too, especially the domesticated ones that are forced to live with chains around their neck and a brand on their forehead. Man separates the males from the females, imposing our human notions and disrupting the natural order. At mating time, my dog goes crazy. All the bitches are locked up behind bars. If some sorry excuse for a 'she' winds up on the street, she's besieged by suitors. When my Caesar comes home I can barely recognize him. Half-bald, with his fur torn up and his eyes all swollen — he looks terrible. If he had a pedigree, people would be fighting over him. Beautiful women, women with lipstick, would refuse me nothing if I would allow my male to fertilize their females."

"Well, well," I say. "What about your cat?"

Ben makes a face. He takes a sip of coffee and clears his throat as if it's hard to talk.

"I had no choice," he says, "but to solve her problem in a brutal fashion. My Princess is no ordinary cat. She traces her lineage to the Persians. She is slender, with a narrow head and the cutest little chin. Her eyes gleam like gold lanterns in her black velvet fur. She never paid attention to the seasons; for her the time was always ripe. I was afraid to let her out — the toms would have torn her to pieces. Poor thing, she couldn't stop begging for what nature demanded. All day she went around with her tail in the air, waiting for a miracle. Eventually I couldn't stand watching her suffer. I took her to a doctor, who killed the phantom supplicant in her blood. Now she's at peace. Fat and lazy. All she does is eat, sleep, wake up and eat again."

Ben sighs. "If only the same could be done to me," he says. He avoids my eyes. "If I were free of physical desire, maybe I would accomplish something, create something that would outlast me after I die. You should see all the unfinished compositions on top of my piano. After I'm gone the janitor will come and throw them all away."

I want to say something to dispel his gloom, but I'm afraid he'll become sentimental. I'm afraid to hear him say he loves me — not because I don't want to hear it, but because I wouldn't be able to say the same back to him, no matter how fervently he wishes I would.

We sit a while longer in strained silence. In the distance, the town clock strikes twelve.

"You must be late for a lesson," I say.

Ben gets up without speaking. He takes a few steps toward the door, then stops and looks back at me. "It's too bad," he says. "Too bad our stars were crossed. Who knows what would have happened if I'd met you twenty years ago?"

I don't answer. I'm not sure exactly what he's thinking, nor do I want to know. In my heart I feel he's not the one who could meet my needs. Just as I am for him, so he is, for me, not the answer but only a temporary refuge.

I look for the answer in yeast yet to rise,
In an astronaut's journey to uncharted skies,
In the shiver I feel when a glance falls on me,
In my shifting emotions — I look for the key.

At times, I find myself thinking in lines of verse. But as soon as I realize I've come up with a poem I hide it under the bed, in hopes that no one will discover it — not even my friend Ben.

OEDIPUS IN BROOKLYN

Sylvia was no Jocasta. She'd never even heard of the Greek tragedies. But fate led her into a narrow strait with no way out. For a while she struggled; then she surrendered to the inevitable. Eyes closed, lips sealed, she yielded to the whims of fortune and said "yes" to the burning "no" inscribed by the ancients in the holy books.

She was twenty-nine years old when she became a widow. One fine Sunday morning, as she busied herself with the housework, her husband took their only child for a ride in his new car. He wanted to demonstrate how rapidly his Chrysler swallowed the miles, how easily it climbed mountains and overtook Cadillacs with the flick of a finger. He was brought home dead. Their nine-year-old son was hospitalized for months and emerged from the operations totally blind.

Sylvia sank into a deep depression. For days she lay in bed with the door closed and shades drawn. She saw no one, spoke to no one, wanted only to die. But the responsibility of caring for her blind son and the benefits issued by the insurance company slowly drew her

out of her lethargy. With the help of psychoanalysis, she began to see
that suicide would not solve her problem. She had eyes; she could find
a way to adapt and understand. She was an adult; the problem was not
herself but her son. It was up to her to find a way to see for them
both — to be his guide, the cane in his hand, the stubborn sunbeam
that cracked the concrete and drew the green sprout up from the deep,
the lone drop of water that nourished the root in the desert. She had
no choice: she was a mother. Providence had so ordained.

Like a wild animal caught in a trap with no hope of escape, Sylvia
began to adjust to her new circumstances. Even in a dungeon, she
told herself, life went on. Even a prisoner on death row found reasons
for optimism.

Sylvia was no stranger to misfortune. In the space of a few months,
she had lost both her parents. Her father's death was as violent and
sudden as her husband's. He was pumping soda water when a man
came into the candy store, asked for an ice cream soda, then ordered
him to open the register and hand over all the cash. When her father
refused, the robber shot him dead.

Sylvia's mother could not bear the blow. Within a year she was
lying beside her husband. By this time Sylvia was engaged. The marriage took place soon after the tragedy with her parents. The young
couple sold the candy store, left the Bronx, and moved to Brooklyn.
They rented an apartment near Prospect Park — new neighbors, a
new world. Here, no one knew about her painful past, and Sylvia was
not inclined to speak of it. She devoted herself to caring for her husband and later to raising their son. With motherly pride she pushed
the stroller along the worn paths in the park. Sitting together on the
benches, she and the other young mothers imagined their children's
future as they played on the grass.

Ten years passed, and then misfortune struck. Now Sylvia understood how her mother had felt. She too wanted to follow her husband

to the grave. But fate denied her that luxury. She had to stay alive for the sake of her son. Danny became the driving force in her life, the electric current that kept her going. She took pleasure in his joys, trembled with his fears, aspired to his hopes, dreamed his dreams, experienced all his childish emotions.

Every morning mother and son went to school together. She sat in a corner and watched the blind children learn to see the world through their fingers. She too began to touch things, to feel with her fingers every obstacle in her path. She even counted the steps between one room and the next. In the evening she refrained from turning on the lights. She set the table, ate dinner, and washed the dishes in the dark. Then mother and son would pass the time with special games: chess for the blind, checkers for the blind. When she got into bed, she would turn on her bedside lamp and lose herself in someone else's life within the pages of a novel.

Danny himself was a voracious reader in Braille. Everything interested him. He still remembered what things had looked like before the light was extinguished, and now he ordered his mother to illuminate the dim fog of his new world, to feed his love of colors and bring them back more vividly than ever. She was to paint for him all the subtle hues in the park as the sun slipped behind the clouds. Hungry for color, he demanded the impossible.

Sylvia struggled to find the required words. Never before had she clothed the world in colors. Now color became the bridge that bound the two of them together.

The boy's sense of smell also intensified. He could predict a change in the weather by sniffing the air, sense the rain hanging in the wind. He could recognize people by the smell of their clothing and even sought to discern their character with his nose.

Danny would stand in front of the mirror and bore into the glass with his sightless eyes. He brushed his hair, patted his face, adjusted his dark glasses. He felt for the crease in his trousers, tried to guess the color of his shoes and socks. Everything had to match — shirt with sweater, sweater with jacket.

When Danny turned thirteen, he tired of the color game. He stopped asking, grew silent and despondent. He couldn't bear conversation and avoided people. Even his mother's voice irritated him; he wanted only quiet. He liked the sound of leaves rustling in the wind. Every day they walked in the park and listened to the cries of the animals at the zoo. Behind the guard's back, they threw peanuts to the monkeys in their cage. Of all the hungry mouths in the park, Danny was especially devoted to the lively squirrels. They waited for him near the Lincoln statue, not far from the kiosk where nuts were sold, and as soon as they picked up his scent they came down from the trees and surrounded him, perched on his shoulders, and emptied his bag.

"They must think I'm a god," Danny remarked one day.

The sudden observation surprised Sylvia and frightened her. She looked at her son with alarm. How had he come up with such an idea? When a blizzard came, Danny insisted on going to the park. He needed to, he said; the squirrels were expecting him.

"In this weather? Let's wait until morning. The snow will have stopped by then."

"If you won't take me, I'll go alone," he insisted.

"Is it so important?"

"Very important. The squirrels mustn't find out that their god is blind."

Danny grew taller and heavier, his muscles covered with a thick layer of fat. The doctor recommended exercises and swimming. "I gather you have no close relatives nearby," he said. "Why not move to a milder climate? Pick a place near the water where your son can burn off some energy."

Sylvia took the doctor's advice. She left Brooklyn, Prospect Park, and the shops and storekeepers of Flatbush Avenue and moved down to Florida.

Danny fell in love with the sea. He swam for hours in the mild, clear turquoise waters of the South Atlantic, drowning his frustrations in the soft arms of the waves. In the evenings he strummed his guitar, expressing the moodiness that had lately overtaken him.

Sylvia sensed danger in his strumming, in his ripe muscles, in the awakening masculinity of his body. She felt it in his silence, his sigh, his casual touch, and never more than when they lay side by side on the sand in the hot sun. Every time they touched, his body trembled. She opened her eyes and saw his muscles straining as he absent-mindedly sifted the hot sand between his fingers.

What Danny was thinking behind his dark glasses she couldn't see — or didn't want to see. As for her own thoughts, the more she tried to sweep them under the rug or hide them under her pillow, the more insistent they became. They winked at her from the foaming waves and from the transistor radio that never stopped yammering, stirring her blood with its songs of love, luck, and sorrow.

When Danny turned sixteen, his mother was thirty-six years old. Men were attracted to her plump, shapely limbs. They showered her with compliments, propositions, promises of paradise on earth. But Danny stood in the way. The local doctor in whom Sylvia confided suggested that she enroll her son in an institution. She must not sacrifice her own life on Danny's account, he said. And Danny himself would benefit. The schools were competent; they would provide him with an opportunity to learn a trade. He would become productive, even independent. He would meet young women in similar circumstances, and in time he would marry and live out his destiny.

Danny rejected the idea out of hand. Every time Sylvia tried to bring it up he became agitated. "I don't want their schools!" he shouted. "I don't want to adjust to their world! Let the world adjust to me!"

Passive by nature, accustomed to bending with the wind, Sylvia did not fight back. The two continued with their daily routine. They delighted in their little house by the sea and enjoyed tending the flowers and shrubs in the garden. Danny's lifetime pension relieved them of worry about the future. Every day they walked into town to buy whatever they needed. Then they bathed in the sea, lay on the beach, and baked in the sun. But this good life quickly became monotonous. Tomorrow was the same as yesterday, yesterday just like today. Time stood still, as if the flora and fauna, the fish of the sea and the birds of the air were imprisoned inside a bubble, man and beast alike forced to take part in the age-old game that Adam and Eve had dreamed up in the Garden of Eden.

All day and all night, fiery instincts seethed within them. Mother and son hid their feelings, concealed their thoughts behind the study of the exotic birds, plants, and ecological characteristics of the semitropical region. Sylvia strove to recreate the strange landscape in Danny's imagination. She painted for him the splendor of the blue heron with its spreading wings, the delicate beauty of the white egret, the ibis with its bill like a spoon. She described the southern mangrove trees whose roots braided whole islands populated by crocodiles, alligators warming themselves in the sun, pink flamingoes watching for fish. The entire area was teeming with life.

"I never heard of these birds," Danny said. "All these plants and animals are too strange. I don't want to hear about them."

Every day Danny became more phlegmatic, unkempt, and preoccupied. For him it was enough to swim and to bake in the sun in silence.

Often some stranger would attach himself to them. Danny couldn't bear the company of these men or the sound of his mother's laughter.

Real and imaginary ailments overtook him: a headache, a stomachache, even a nervous case of the hiccups provided an excuse to leave.

On the way home, Danny would insist that they make a detour or lose themselves within the crowd in a shop before heading back to the house.

"You have eyes," he argued. "I have to make sure no one is following us. You might be giving a signal so you can run off with him. Maybe you want to get rid of me."

It wasn't only jealousy that tormented Danny. He was truly afraid of strangers. He didn't trust the sighted world. After each such encounter he would walk around the house sniffing the air for unfamiliar scents. Nor did sleep bring peace to his jangled nerves. He cried out and woke himself with his screams.

During one such night of troubled sleep, Danny opened the door to his mother's room, felt his way to her side, and patted the blanket. He had dreamed that a man was in bed with her.

Frightened, Sylvia encircled him with her bare arms and tried to soothe him. He was trembling. She moved over in the bed to make room for him. He nestled into her arms and buried his head in her soft bosom. The silky folds of her nightgown cooled his face. He breathed in the scent of the lotion she had rubbed into her skin. Under cover of night, intoxicated with her rich femininity, his body became aroused, hot and demanding. The rhythm in his blood sought and found the narrow route to the open sea. Without words, without caresses, as mute and urgent as a magic incantation, he took her.

Sylvia did not resist the stormy rhythm. Deep within the river of her femininity she remembered other rhythms, other embraces in which she'd engaged as an active partner with her husband. She remembered words that had stirred her blood, penetrated to the depths of her being. Now she pressed her ear to her son's mouth, but no words came — only the hot, mute plea of a thirsty man in the desert.

Sylvia did not muster the power or will to repel this desperate assault. She persuaded herself that she was lying not with her son but with the specter of her husband. A power stronger than death had broken through the barrier between this world and that, and in the form of her son had come to demand the debt she owed to his unlived life.

That summer the heat was intense. A blinding haze hung in the air like carbon fumes. The earth was scorched, the waterways dried up, the white egrets disappeared. The roots of the mangrove trees, naked and greedy, waited for a drop of water. Creeping insects of all kinds eked out their slithery existence, leaving behind silver threads of slime on the desiccated waterbed.

Only the sea in its stoic indifference did not cease its endless song.

The brief tropical rains failed to cool the atmosphere. Buckets of rain would fall, and a moment later the sun would come out, dry up the puddles, and thicken the heavy air. The heat weighed on the spirit and muddled common sense. Nor did the sea soothe the spirit; its salts and minerals scalded the skin and drove people from the water.

Sylvia and Danny hid from the sun. In the house, the air conditioner cooled their parched bodies. Mute, without words, without tenderness, without promise, without hope, they coupled day and night — on the floor, and after sunset on the hot sand.

Under the press of the tropical sun, their ingrained Jewish modesty evaporated. All that remained was the naked kernel of lust. In the thick mist of that summer, even instinct veered off course. Nature played tricks with her own taboo — and Sylvia discovered that she was pregnant. She did not tell her son. She didn't even try to think about the tragedy of her situation. She knew she could have an abortion. The doctor would ask no questions. For a few hundred dollars he would sharpen his scissors and poke at her womb and the nightmare would trickle out. But Sylvia did nothing. She relied on nature in its wisdom to take its course. The same power that had led her into the mire would lead her out again.

Once while Sylvia and Danny were walking along the shore, he grew suddenly loquacious.

"Have you ever read the Bible?" he asked.

"No," Sylvia replied.

"You must have heard of Adam and Eve," he said. "Why do you think Cain murdered his brother Abel? I'll tell you: it was jealousy, pure and simple. The two brothers both wanted their mother, and they both gave her presents. Cain, the farmer, brought her the sweetest fruit of the earth, and Abel, the shepherd, gave his youngest and fattest sheep. And when Cain found out that Eve liked Abel's gift better than his, he picked up a scythe and murdered his brother."

"How do you know all this?"

"I know a lot of things," Danny said, "more than you think. You think I'm just a blind cripple. But actually my blindness helps me see better, much better. Sometimes I feel like my own creator, even my own god. I can feel a cosmic power running through, pushing me to create my own world, to go looking for the secret of all secrets. You can't possibly understand — you don't want to. Maybe I don't even understand myself, but I have a feeling I'm on the right path, and that's all that matters."

Sylvia could not grasp what Danny was saying, nor did she try. The world of rock and roll had hypnotized her. The barbaric rhythm afforded her a secret passage to no-man's land, far removed from the problems of the real world. The pictures conjured by the music called to her spirit and filled every cell in her body with restless longing. Just as the tropical rain did not cool the air, so was Sylvia unable to still her boiling blood. She began to feel like a burden on Danny. Often he would take the dog and slip out of the house, leaving her alone until late at night.

At times like this Sylvia would lie still, staring at the wall and waiting. She closed her eyes and imagined that she, too, was blind: she neither saw nor knew what was required of her. She lay as motionless as a mite in the sand, inhaling her own stale aroma and the perfume of her hair that spilled across the pillow like golden apple cider.

The jungle beat of the rock and roll music pounded on. Over and over, it happened: two bodies joined together, sensing each other's demands like telephone antennae and yielding without a word. Maybe they remained silent for fear of awakening reality, as if some magical spirit would be roused and vanish into nothing with a snap of the fingers, like the prince in the fairy tale.

Both of them wanted to prolong the moment. Perhaps they wanted to trick the laws of nature into standing still — unaware that nature does not allow anything to remain static. Even the riverbed changes its course, mountains erupt, and tiny particles of coral rise out of the abyss to form new continents.

Perhaps Danny did not know his mother was pregnant. Or perhaps he was waiting for her to tell him. Sylvia said nothing as she felt the rising life wriggling within her, knocking on the wall of her being, demanding its right to exist.

When the first pains impinged on her consciousness, Sylvia opened her eyes and looked around in surprise, as if she had no idea what could be causing them.

It was the middle of the night. The house was pitch black. She rose from her bed. Barefoot, wearing only her nightgown, she went out into the street.

A low sky hung over the sea. The Milky Way parted the darkness in two. From time to time a star slipped and fell into the ocean. The sea accepted everything. In the same stoical manner as always, it continued to sing its intrinsic song, just as it had day in and day out, year in and year out, all through the ages.

Sylvia walked far out along the water's edge toward the seawall where she and Danny had often sat. She liked to dabble her feet in the cool water and watch the sea crabs hurrying in and out of nooks and crannies.

Once she had picked up one of these crabs and laid it in Danny's hand. Danny had played with the crab, had asked how many feet it had and what it looked like. Was it a male or a female?

"Hard to know," Sylvia answered.

"Maybe it doesn't know either," Danny said. "Why should it? It's only a pawn on the evolutionary chessboard. We are, too — toys in the hands of fortune, nature's experiment with something new. I know, Sylvia, I can feel it, I can see what other people can't. Look at this crab; it's as blind as I am, but blindness tells it where to go. It never gets lost. It never has doubts. It knows what's a dream and what's reality."

"What is reality?" Sylvia asked.

Danny didn't answer right away. He took off his dark glasses and polished them with care. Only when they were perched on his nose once again did he reply with a flourish.

"You want to know what is real? Why do you need to? Do you think if you know you'll be worth more than a crab? Well, you're wrong."

"A crab doesn't have to pay for its sins," Sylvia interrupted him. "A person does."

Danny's face reddened with anger. "What's the matter with you? How do you think you've sinned? Anyway, there's no such thing as sin. Only Man suffers from such a disease. When it comes time to pay,

I'll get in line ahead of you. And I'll have some questions, too — if there's anyone to ask."

Now Sylvia ran to the seawall where they often sat. The pains resumed, sharper and more frequent than before. She ran along the white foam at the water's edge and tried to scramble up onto the rock where she had once scratched her name. But her bare feet slipped and she stumbled and fell headfirst into the water. For a while she struggled against the morning tide. She tried to cry out, but the incoming water filled her mouth. A high wave rushed in. It lifted up her velvet-smooth body, battered it from side to side, threw it on its back and pulled it deeper into the sea. The wave rocked her back and forth, toying with her. It lifted her nightgown, loosened her hair. Another wave rushed in and slammed her back onto the beach. Her protruding belly jabbed against a sharp stone.

The morning sun found Sylvia lying face up beside the stone wall. A flock of pelicans with baggy throats pecked avidly at her open belly. Exotic seaweed transported from distant lands tangled in her apple-cider hair. Nimble sea creatures explored her silky body. Up above, gray-white vultures searching for carrion circled with raucous cries. Not quite ready to claim their prey, they settled onto the sun-splashed stone bridge and patiently awaited their turn.

COUSIN CLAUDE

My husband tossed the newspaper across the table. "Your 'cousin' is having another exhibit," he said. The cup of coffee in my hand began to tremble. The scornful word "cousin" made me angry. It didn't exactly apply to Claude. Within the family we had always avoided specifying his exact relationship to us. Claude was like a weed, borne by the wind into our tidy garden.

Once, during some childhood argument, I'd shouted the word in his face: "Cousin! Cousin!" I don't know how, but I knew it was the cruelest lash I could use against him.

Claude said nothing in response. He just stood there, paralyzed. His eyes flamed black and his lips turned white, drained of blood. He looked at me, or, more precisely, over me, somewhere off into the distance, and started banging his head against the wall, as if it weren't actually his head at all, but the head of some venomous reptile that had just injected him with poison.

That evening Claude didn't come to dinner. He lay in bed with his eyes closed and refused to speak. I shut my bedroom door, too, on the pretext that I had a lot of homework. I opened a book and looked at the words without understanding what I was reading. That night I vowed never again to use the word with regard to him. Whenever a girlfriend asked "Is that your cousin?" my heart would stop.

For the ten years that we lived under the same roof, he was Claude, neither cousin nor brother, simply Claude. Claude, with all his faults and strengths, his contradictions and his complexes: Claude.

Now, as I heard the word at breakfast, I felt at once offended and proud. I could hear the sarcastic dig in my husband's tone. He loved to go on about how Claude was nothing more than a graffiti artist. New York was full of them, he said. All the subway cars were adorned with their scribbles.

"Well, I'm going to his show," I said, more out of spite than anything else.

"Did he invite you?"

"I don't need an invitation from my own brother."

"He's your cousin, not your brother," my husband said.

"He is what he is," I retorted. "He's a human being, an artist. He's Claude, that's all!"

My husband didn't respond. He picked up his briefcase and left the house. Alone with my thoughts, I took out my rage on the housework. I ran the vacuum cleaner through every room, shouting at the top of my lungs: Why do you have to label people like cans at the grocery store? Anyone who lives through so much and stays true to himself is worth more than some two-bit lawyer who makes a living off of other people's suffering. He's a bigger man than you!

Having said my piece, I felt better. I turned on the radio, then turned it off. Did he remember me the way I remembered him? Did I figure in any of his paintings? What was his work about?

A friend called to invite me to lunch. I said yes, even though I knew I wouldn't go. My thoughts were racing in every direction. Past and present mingled, then merged. I could see the *Atom II*, the ship that brought Claude to America. The day was etched in my memory like an illustrated calendar. The mood at home, the weather, the mist that hung over Prospect Park, even the way the air smelled on that late summer day had never left me.

On the day of Claude's arrival my older brother and I didn't go to school. Mother made up a bed for him in my brother's room. My bed and books were moved into the dining room. Every corner of the house radiated expectation. The floors gleamed with a new coat of wax. The curtains were freshly ironed. There were flowers on the table and a sponge cake in the refrigerator.

My mother didn't stop talking about Claude, his parents, and their elegant residence in Paris, with its crystal lamps and expensive carpets. By the time he was five, Claude was taller than my brother, who was one year older. The more my mother said about him, the taller Claude grew in my mind.

I created a variety of images of him, depending on my mood. I played with his likeness as if with a doll, dressing him in fantastic costumes with feathers and ribbons and patent leather shoes. My nine-year-old imagination could not be contained. I looked up to Claude with fear and love. And the more attractive I made him, the uglier I found myself.

Anything and everything French was placed on a pedestal in our house. We couldn't admire a local landscape without having my mother compare it unfavorably to the French countryside. French food, French clothes, French culture . . . nostalgia hung like a pall over our heads.

When the horrific news began to arrive from across the ocean, however, my mother changed her attitude toward the French and all of Europe. She became active in relief organizations and took part in school activities to help refugee children feel more at home in a strange world.

The day of Claude's arrival was bright and sunny. Our taxi sped through unfamiliar streets, all of us silently urging it to go even faster.

As we approached the harbor, I grew terrified. What would he think of me? What kind of impression would I make? How would I measure up against the Parisian girls? I searched for my reflection in the taxi window, but what I saw — two thin braids with red ribbons framing my face — made me even more distraught. For the first time in my life I hated my mother for dressing me like the child I was.

I huddled close to my father, hoping for a compliment, but he ignored me. All of us sat in strained, tense silence.

When we finally reached the port, we found the *Atom II* anchored there — a pitiful little ship with peeling gray paint and a yellow and red smokestack. It was dwarfed by the giant *Queen Mary* in the next berth.

At the sight of multitudes streaming out of the ship, my spirits fell. An agent of HIAS, the Hebrew Immigrant Aid Society, assured us that a passenger by the name of Claude Kohn was indeed on board, but because of the large number of passengers and the incompetence of the French company, it would take a while for everyone to disembark. Not permitted to board the ship to look for him, we started calling out in unison "Claude! Claude!" while scanning the crowd.

Finally a little boy appeared at the end of the gangplank. A black beret was pulled down over his ears. He wore short pants and no socks. Instead of a shirt, a torn sweater covered his narrow shoulders, from which a brown backpack hung open and empty.

"*Mon dieu!*" my mother cried. "That must be Claude!"

Claude looked down at his torn shoes without saying a word. My father reached out and lifted him up as if he were a very small child.

Before us stood a neglected, emaciated little boy who gave off an acrid stench of sweat and filth.

"I'll sue!" my father fumed. "Is this any way to treat a child? I pay good money for his fare and they cram in a thousand people like sardines. How dare they?"

My mother covered her eyes and wept silently. The agent from HIAS came running. He steered us through customs, wished us well, and presented Claude with a little leather pouch with his name engraved in gold letters. Inside was a crisp new dollar bill.

Claude stared at the pouch with shining eyes. He inspected it from all sides, stroked it, laid it against his face. At first he didn't know where to put it, but then he remembered his backpack. Quickly he stowed the little pouch inside, then offered a hand to each of us in turn.

"*Ça va?*"

"*Ça va très bien!*" we responded, and took Claude home with us. My mother bathed him and dressed him in clean clothes. Everything he was wearing went into the trash. But Claude would not be parted from his backpack. He hung it on the wall above his bed, and there it remained.

The next day was the Sabbath. The boy who'd been our cousin became our brother. So my father solemnly pronounced at the kitchen table as my mother served hot pancakes with honey, butter, milk, and several kinds of jam.

When Claude ignored his fork and helped himself with his fingers, my brother burst out laughing. Claude stared at him and continued as before.

He wanted to know why we didn't boil our milk but drank it straight from the bottle, and why there was no wine on the table. He told us about his experiences on the ship. When there was a storm and everyone was sick, he'd stayed on deck and helped the sailors sweep off the water. The sailors treated him well. When he grew up, he too would be a sailor. He'd had many things in his backpack, among them his father's gold watch — the peasant woman who'd hidden him had allowed him to keep it. But one night while he slept someone had stolen it. At this point, Claude showed us bruises from the fights he'd had with those he'd accused of the theft.

While Claude was speaking, I enjoyed looking at his perfect white teeth, his charming smile, his velvety black hair. I saw that the skin on his face and neck was studded with abrasions, both large and small.

After breakfast my father stood up. He asked the rest of us to remain seated, then rubbed his hands together and paced back and forth, searching for words. He cleared his throat and gave a passionate speech.

"From now on," he told Claude, "I am your father, she is your mother, he is your brother, and she is your sister."

After that we all stood up and kissed one other ceremonially in the French manner, twice on each cheek, and furtively wiped away our tears.

———

Claude adapted quickly to his new way of life. He liked his new clothes, even though it was hard to get used to wearing long pants and going without the smock he'd worn at his French school. He was thrilled with his new shoes and even enjoyed how they squeaked. He had his own corner for his things and rearranged them every day, taking note of each new item. Every day he added something he'd found in the street: a book, a pencil, a penny.

One day he found a dollar, which he put in his pouch with the one from HIAS. The pouch lay in a little gilded box tied with a silk ribbon. He kept it in his dresser along with his parents' wedding portrait.

Above all else, Claude treasured his sailor's cap, even though, in keeping with the sailor tradition, it caused him more trouble than joy.

As soon as they caught wind of an outsider, the children on the street banded together to attack him. First they tore off his hat, as if it were Samson's locks, and then they forced him to repeat filthy words and write them on the sidewalk with chalk. To get the cap back, he had to translate the words into French. But Claude took his revenge by aiming the abusive words at his tormentors as he wrote.

The more grief the cap caused him, the more attached to it he became. The cap made him seem taller and lent him an air of importance. He wore it sideways, on the crown of his head, or pulled down over his eyes. It became his signature look. Even from a distance there was no mistaking him. His best friends couldn't resist the temptation; at the slightest disagreement the cap flew into the gutter.

Every time Claude came home with dirt on his hat, he refused to eat supper. He lay in bed with stomach cramps or a headache. But over time his ailments abated. His scratched face cleared. His fair complexion set off his dazzling black eyes and even blacker hair.

The poison in his skin had entered his bloodstream, and from time to time abscesses swelled on his body. Large doses of vitamin B slowly healed these sores, but while the poison dissolved chemically, it transformed itself into something that could not be cured by vitamins, something that settled into the dark corners of his soul, in the deep recesses where the self rules with an iron hand, forcing each of us to stay true to our essential nature.

Once, while making his bed, my mother discovered under the mattress a cache of children's rifles, plastic revolvers, pocket knives, and clay soldiers, all purchased at the five-and-dime store.

Upon investigation it emerged that Claude had joined a street gang that protected him from attack — for a certain price. Neither my father's beatings nor my mother's entreaties could persuade him to reveal the gang's identity. Having pledged himself to secrecy, he locked his lips and threw away the key.

The gang was not his only problem. In school he had been placed in a class with children three years younger, which he found mortifying. He skipped school whenever he could. When he did go, he would sit and draw pictures instead of listening to the teacher.

After the New Year, Claude was promoted to a higher grade, and this marked a turning point. All of a sudden he began to speak English. He abandoned his French so completely that by the time spring came he wouldn't speak it at all, claiming that he'd forgotten it. He was proud of his English and was no longer afraid of making mistakes that would cause people to laugh at him — as they had at Sunday school soon after he arrived. Having seen the word "women" on the restroom door, he'd raised his hand and asked to go to the "women." The children had burst out laughing, and their mockery had imprinted itself on his soul.

Learning English didn't solve all of Claude's problems. He didn't always feel like part of the family. Awake or asleep, he was tormented by nightmares. He would measure with his eyes the meat on my brother's plate, and even though he could never finish his own portion, it bothered him that my brother received more. At night he cried out in his sleep and often ran to touch his pouch, which by now was crammed with dollar bills. The pouch became a kind of idol, an altar upon which he sacrificed the weekly allowance he was given for buying ice cream, chocolate, or the movies he so loved.

The parents in the photo on his wall and the parents he lived with at home — our parents — were not at peace within him. Hatred and love warred within him. He found fault in the harsh words of his teacher, in a misunderstanding with a friend, in my brother's strong muscles, in my playing the piano, and he fought back with the only weapons he had. He threw my doll in the trash and slashed my brother's boxing glove, forcing us to regard him as an intruder demanding equal rights in alien territory.

As soon as Claude started high school he discovered what my parents had tried to hide from him. He threw himself into reading books about the Holocaust.

Now, suddenly, he remembered his French. He read his parents' letters, then hid them among his things. Everything that had to do with his parents, he hid. He wrote down the date and place where his father was shot. He resumed contact with the French family from whose house his mother had been deported. In a notebook in the pouch from HIAS, he recorded his old address in Paris along with those of friends who had survived. By now his dollars had been deposited in the bank; the gilded box was no longer of any importance to him.

On his dresser now lay magazines and clippings of models, both clothed and nude. In his free time he would draw whatever came into his hands. He'd put the head of one girl on the body of another. Sometimes I'd recognize one of my dresses on the body of a film actress.

My relationship with Claude grew increasingly strained. Every innocent touch elicited feelings that secretly scared us both. At night in bed, and when I got dressed or undressed, I was afraid.

I've never forgotten how his hand strayed over my body on the night of the fire. In the middle of the night, we were awakened and led out of the house in our underwear. We were given blankets and escorted to the temple nearby, where we lay down on benches and tried to sleep.

A narrow table stood between us. Wrapped in his blanket, Claude slipped off the bench and began his assault. I lay without moving, pretending I was asleep. Afraid to say anything, afraid to fan the flames, I allowed his hand to wander. From time to time I stirred as if I were about to wake up, then fell back under his spell.

At daybreak we returned home. Things were no longer the same between us. We avoided speaking to each other or making eye contact. He never approved of the boys I brought home, nor I of his girls. Still, having tested our fireworks on each other, we were glad to go our separate ways.

After high school, Claude joined the navy. For three years he sailed all over the world, visiting places he wanted to see and meeting people he wanted to talk to. What he learned from these experiences he kept to himself.

When Claude returned, I was a married woman. Over the years he had matured, grown taller. His gaze was deeper, more enigmatic. Only his smile with its flashing white teeth remained the same — open-hearted and full of charm.

He didn't stay at home for long. He took the pouch with his name in gold letters, by then nearly illegible. He dusted off his brown back-pack and filled it with the things with which he had a kind of mystical connection, a soulful bond that did not need to be put into words.

We seldom heard from him. On holidays he sent a card with a drawing appropriate to the occasion. He said little about himself. Not from him but from reading a San Francisco-based magazine we learned that he'd become a successful painter. One of his shows won high acclaim.

As the years passed, Claude remained the forbidden tree in the middle of my carpeted Garden of Eden. Over the noise of the vacuum cleaner my personal antennae sought a connection. Perhaps with him things could have been different, I thought. Perhaps the two of us could have attained a more authentic life together. Perhaps with each other we would have managed to avoid the trap of an empty paradise. Perhaps we could have forged a more fundamental inner truth. Perhaps . . .

Just before calling home to tell my mother the news about Claude's exhibit, I went to the mailbox and found a letter from California, an illustrated invitation from him. On the cover was a lithograph, a portrait of a little girl. Her thin braids tied with red ribbons and her two frightened eyes took up more than half of her face. She was looking at a ship in the port, and her ribbons were reaching out toward it. They came close, very close, but they never quite touched the ship.

A Yiddish Poet in Paris

It was because of a poem that Sumer Gottlieb came to live in Belleville. His first home in Paris had been in the Latin Quarter, not far from the Sorbonne, where he had studied medicine.

The medical profession had been his mother's idea. She had insisted that he become a doctor, a healer of the sick, and in that way honor the memory of his father, who had died young, a victim of consumption.

Gottlieb greeted the challenges that came his way with youthful enthusiasm. He worked and studied hard; his mother sent small sums of money. Even when he didn't have enough to eat, he took his misfortune in stride.

Once, when his mother's check was delayed and his growling stomach made it impossible to focus on his medical studies, he took a blank sheet of paper and in a florid script set down some short lines in Yiddish — lines that shone, flooding the pages with visions of rye bread spread with fresh butter. He arranged the bread on a tray and placed it at the very tip of the Eiffel Tower. At the foot of the Tower, flowers bloomed and pruned willows formed geometric patterns. Pretty young ladies strolled along the avenues. A scrawny little boy in short pants and no socks squinted up at the bread, and with the insouciance of Victor Hugo's Gavroche he stuck out his parched tongue.

A Yiddish journal published the poem. He received no payment, but the poem did lead to a job: he was awarded a position at a Yiddish print shop in the heart of Belleville. Sumer Gottlieb left the Sorbonne and the Latin Quarter and went to live in the Hotel Nationale.

It was a radical change. His new surroundings were more Warsaw than Paris. Here where Eastern European immigrants had found refuge, young men and women shared their problems, their successes, and their failures. Fellow countrymen helped one another to obtain a small loan or find the address of a hustler who could turn the illegal into the legitimate. A variety of accents resounded in the stairwells, all the way up to the sixth floor. Gottlieb's room on the second floor became a kind of meeting place for the "intelligentsia." Those who lived on the upper floors liked to stop in, open their paper bags, wolf down a quick supper of bread and cheese, and then return to the evening boulevards to search for a few moments of love.

Hanke, who lived on the sixth floor, was a frequent visitor. She would put down her packages, borrow a book, or listen to the poem that Gottlieb had selected to read aloud.

On Sundays the Hotel Nationale rested. Workers turned off their alarm clocks and slumbered in God's embrace. Nor did Sumer Gottlieb rush to rise from his bed. He loved to burrow in his early morning dreams. On this Sunday he dreamed he was standing before a row of colorful neckties, determined to find one to wear at the writers' banquet. He wanted to look through the ties to see what he might choose, but his hands were limp, as if completely paralyzed. A well-dressed salesman with pomaded hair and pressed trousers was making him feel small. The man was impatient; he had to be somewhere, he said. "What's taking you so long?" he demanded. "They're locking up. You don't intend to stay all night, do you?"

Gottlieb pried his eyes open. The room was full of the golden light of spring. The acacia tree, decked out like a bride on her wedding day, looked in at him through the window. Gottlieb yawned, covered his head, and went back to sleep. Before long he was back at the neckties. Hanke was with him, helping him select the right one. Although her voice was quiet and unassuming, she insisted on arguing with everything he said. If he said the red tie would be good with the blue suit, she stared at him as if he'd declared himself to be as strong as Samson. If he suggested the blue one with the little white flowers, she burst out laughing in a way that was completely out of character. Her laughter made him go hot and cold. Was she flirting with him? He felt her breath on his face. His throat constricted. An erotic shiver coursed through him. He breathed with difficulty, gasping for air. He wanted to pull back, to free himself from her provocative closeness, but she insisted that he try on the tie. It's pure silk, she said. How could it be silk, if it felt so scratchy? The knot tightened around his neck. Any tighter and it would strangle him. Gottlieb awakened again. He sat up and convulsed in a fit of dry coughing.

It was nearly noon when Gottlieb got out of bed. He stuffed his feet into his slippers and went into the bathroom, where he lathered his face and stood at the mirror making plans for the first beautiful spring day. Certainly it would be good to sit down and write, the way he had done all winter. But on an extraordinarily beautiful day like this, it was a sin to sit inside. How could one not go outside to greet such an unsullied sky, such fresh sunshine? The air, saturated with the scent of white snowdrops, excited his senses and aroused his emotions.

Gottlieb finished shaving. When he returned to his bedroom, he noticed the red tie hanging on a chair next to the bed. He stood for a moment, lost in thought. The dream came to him, with all its complex sensations, hidden desires, and contradictions. And why not — he asked himself — why on earth shouldn't he invite the delicate young woman from the sixth floor to spend the afternoon with him? A tragi-comic situation, thought Gottlieb, that he needed a dream to tell him what to do. Everything in him seethed with anticipation. He wasn't sure quite what he was expecting, but he hoped to go where only a select few had gone before.

The young leaves of the acacia tree stirred in a golden-green dream. Surely a creative person had to be free from obligations, from familial ties, from diapers and children. One's first love had to be the muse, and yet such literary giants as Bialik, Peretz, and Leivick had managed to raise families without stunting their talent.

Thinking about marriage, Gottlieb remembered Czuda, the Hungarian student he'd gone out with. A spirited girl, a nymphomaniac par excellence. Her golden eyes had emitted a phosphorescent glow in the dark. Like a tigress in heat, she had ordered him around day and night. Yet now he longed to flirt with the underdeveloped mademoiselle from the sixth floor. She baffled him. One moment she was so friendly, other times so silent, despondent, miles away. Her appearance, too, changed from beautiful to ugly, then back again. Her head on its white neck looked like a tulip in the snow. The unexpected metaphor surprised him. Soon thereafter came a second and a third. Poetic visions crashed through dams. Words arranged themselves in rhymes. Gottlieb swam in a sea of exalted lines, then burst into a sudden fit of coughing that extinguished the poetic fireworks. He spat and clutched his heart, as he always did at the sight of blood, as though he wanted instinctively to hack a path to the serpent's nest, grab hold of the monster housed in his lung and choke it to death.

It was all his mother's fault. She had insisted on making a doctor out of him. Nothing else was good enough for her. A carpenter, a tailor, a pickpocket — no, her son had to be a doctor. He had to redeem her hard labor as a charcoal dealer, her soot-blackened face that did not come clean even in her Friday afternoon bath. "So, Mother, look at your son now, your son the doctor, your only child, who will say Kaddish for you when you die. See how he wrestles with the Angel of Death, watch him spitting up phlegm, spitting up life itself. . . . And you, Mother, you're still living in a fairy tale."

After a glass of cold water, Gottlieb felt calmer. He stood by the window and looked within himself. If Hanke were here with him, he would feel better, he thought. A person was not, after all, a stone or a tree. Did trees also suffer from consumption? O, just God, see how the blossoms fall to the ground. Dear white seeds, what do you want from life? A clot of earth? A drop of water? A ray of sun? Don't hurry, darlings, all that awaits you here are stones, stones.

Gottlieb stood for a long time by the window, searching for a way to express what he was feeling. The blue sky became overcast with gray mist. A wind came out of nowhere, and the blossoms drifted down. He turned from the window, and as he did every Sunday, sat down to write his weekly letter to his mother.

> *Dear Mama,*
>
> *Don't worry so much. All is well here. I work during the day and study in the evening. I hope I'll soon make you a mother-in-law. Don't worry, Mama, she's a Jewish girl in every way. I'll give you more details in my next letter. Stay well. Don't work too hard, and don't keep me waiting for your next letter.*
>
> *Love always,*
> *Your Sumer*

After sealing the envelope, he felt ashamed. "What is the matter with me? Why I am lying? Why am I fooling myself and my mother?

I close my eyes and believe I'm invisible. For whom am I pretending? And to what end? The joke is on me, and what a bloody joke it is."

Church bells were ringing nearby. To Gottlieb they sounded different from the bells in Warsaw. There the bells echoed with fear, with dread and the gentile's animosity toward the Jew. As a boy, he would stuff his ears so as not to hear the impure sound. Gottlieb closed his eyes. Memories came flooding in. His thoughts became jumbled, images crisscrossed and chased one other. Felke, a girlfriend from his youth, looked at him with sad eyes. She knew that he would never come back to her. Her sorrow pained him. He wanted to retain the image there at the train station. He wanted to press it like roses in the book of memory.

On the table lay a notebook, a pen, and an eraser. Gottlieb picked up his writing implements and got into bed. The pen flew from line to line as if of its own accord. He didn't look at the clock and so didn't notice that the day was disappearing. Poetry streamed from hidden sources, page after page. All day Gottlieb wrote and wrote. Only when the tree was enveloped in night shadows did he stop to read what he'd written. He read it once, then again. He tried to think of a title for the new poem, but his mind was depleted. While preparing his meal at the stove, he put down as an afterthought the following heading: "The Independent Life of the Other Self."

One fine Saturday afternoon in late autumn, Hanke stood before the mirror getting ready for a date. First she tried out the new hairdo that was taking the mid-Thirties by storm. Once the look was complete, she trained a critical eye on the towering head of hair and decided that what had worked for Madame Pompadour did not work for her. After undoing the complex tangle, she made a part in the middle that allowed her dark hair to fall freely, framing her profile with a single lock posed like question mark on her forehead. So she had looked when Jacques had first seen her, and so she would remain. In her mind, she could see the broad grin and twinkling eye that showed that he agreed with her. All day, all night, his gaze followed her to and from work, up to her garret lodgings. He looked out at her from every nook and cranny, and spoke to her, too: "You don't trust me, Hanke, do you?" His French accent stirred her fantasies. She twisted the lock on her forehead and smiled at his words: "This lock is driving me crazy," he was saying, "and you're laughing?" "I'm laughing because I'm happy," she answered in her mind. "I love you, but — " "But what?" he said and gave her a kiss right in the middle of the street. French passersby understood and smiled knowingly. What was important was the moment, the kiss, the stroll along the Seine, the star rising above Notre Dame.

Standing before the mirror, she remembered it all: the blind musician on the café terrace, the jingle of the coin that she had thrown into his money box, and the secret wish that went along with it.

A knock interrupted her thoughts. Someone was pushing a note under her door. Hanke looked at the note: Jacques! Something had happened to Jacques. No, in fact it was from Sumer Gottlieb. Dear God, what did he want from her? She unfolded the note. Yiddish letters ran before her eyes: "Dear one, please be so good as to give me a few minutes of your time. I have a problem and must speak to you as soon as possible."

Hanke stood with the note in her hand. She could certainly find an excuse: she could say she hadn't found the note until Sunday morning. Whatever happened, she mustn't spoil her date. She had too many hopes riding on it. She grabbed her coat and purse and ran down the stairs. On the second floor, she paused. I must look in on him, she thought, just for a minute. Jacques will wait. He must wait. He must . . .

Hanke found Gottlieb in bed. Half sitting, half lying, he was propped up by a mountain of pillows. Silently, he extended two damp hands to her. The tears in his eyes spoke for him.

"*Comment ça va?*" Hanke asked reflexively.

"Have a seat. We can chat for a bit."

Hanke sat down on a chair by the bed.

"You must certainly be busy on a Saturday night, no? Please excuse me for taking your time."

"My time should not concern you," she replied. "Your situation is what matters now."

Gottlieb was silent. The room was full of evening shadows. A heavy mist rose from the vaporizer. The steam curled and uncurled in unusual forms. On the bookcase, clowns were grinding their black teeth. On the bare tree branches, monsters with enormous heads and long tails were rocking back and forth. The bowl by Gottlieb's bed was full of red phlegm.

"So this is it!" Hanke thought. She was embarrassed by her own good health, by her white blouse and the lock on her forehead. She went to the window and furtively wiped off her lipstick and pushed the lock off her brow.

"Can I make you a glass of tea?" she asked.

"Yes, why not?" Gottlieb answered.

Hanke tiptoed as if she were being careful not to wake herself. The glasses were so greasy that they slipped in her hands. Was he aware of his condition? she wondered. Did he know how things stood? What did a person think when he saw death before his very eyes? Did he complain to God, to fate? What use was knowing when one could do nothing about it?

Gottlieb looked at Hanke, sorry not to have seen her like this before, so warm and helpful. Perhaps his mind was clouded by memories of the other girl, the tigress? The problem with Hanke was that she was so closed, so aloof and cold. In metaphor he saw her as if in an old-fashioned ballad, in which pious grandmothers stood guard at the door. She lacked the élan, the self-confidence of a modern woman.

Hanke brought him the glass of tea. Her breasts under the white blouse seemed to grow larger before his eyes. Gottlieb felt as if his very muscles were reveling in the sight.

"Come, Hanke, sit next to me," he said. "Even tea is better drunk in pairs."

Hanke tried to smile. Everything inside her was weeping. Why couldn't this have happened yesterday or the day before? Why today of all days? She sat down like a condemned person awaiting sentence. Of course she could still save herself, escape from the morbid scene. If she stayed, something terrible was bound to happen. She could tell by the avid look in his eyes and his quickening breath. She sat staring into space as if nailed to the chair. She seemed to see the earth opening up and was too terrified to budge.

Gottlieb could sense her embarrassment. "It's not too early to recite the end-of-Sabbath prayer and light the candles," he said. "Have you ever read 'The Golden Chain' by Peretz? Remember how Shloyme wanted to prolong the Sabbath? That was so long ago. Have you read Peretz?"

"Who?"

"I. L. Peretz."

"I think so, but I don't remember."

"Forgive me, dear Hanke. I know I'm forcing myself on you, keeping you here against your will. Unfortunately, that's how sick people are. As soon as they sense that their condition is critical, they become egocentric; they don't have eyes for anyone except themselves."

He laughed nervously, took her hand in his own and stroked it for a long time.

"If I'm not mistaken," he said after a while, "we'll have a full moon tonight. I'm not sure, though. I haven't made such romantic calculations lately. You know what I mean. I feel terribly guilty that you're suffering here because of me. I mean, if a healthy young man is waiting for you, go and enjoy life." Gottlieb broke into a dry cough and fell silent.

Hanke too was silent. She felt as if she were sinking into a quagmire of pity. Yellow-gray and stiff as parchment, his face contorted. White foam formed at the sides of his mouth, and his eyes were full of humility. She wanted to tell him that she hadn't earned his admiration, that she was not who he thought she was. That she had gotten entangled with a Frenchman and God only knew where that would lead.

"I don't have a date," she said. "No one is waiting for me. If you'll let me, I'll make you something to eat."

"No, my darling, I'm really not hungry," he said. "All I want is to look at you and perhaps talk a little."

"I see that your pantry is bare. I can run down and buy something for you, perhaps a cold lemonade?"

"No, sit, my darling, don't trouble yourself. The Angel of Death will soon see to everything I need."

Now that the quicksand had swallowed her completely, there was nothing to fear. Her tongue loosened.

"Sumer Gottlieb," she said, "you're speaking foolishness. It's totally inappropriate for a medical student."

"I'm not a student anymore. I'm a worker."

"All right — a worker. So what? Nowadays they manage to cure the most complicated illnesses. And better working conditions help, too — now that there are Saturdays off and higher wages."

"I don't have anything to do with these positive developments," Gottlieb interrupted her. "I have dropped out of the ranks."

"I don't understand."

"All right, I'll explain," he said. "I no longer go to work. Doctor's orders."

"Well then, change your job. The kind of work you do must be harmful to your health."

"Even breathing is harmful for someone without lungs."

Hanke was at a loss for words again. She began to busy herself with the housework. She washed the dishes and gathered up the old magazines. It was already dark outside. The bedside lamp illuminated half of the room; the other half was bathed in darkness. The tree outside was also wrapped in black. Hanke thought she saw Jacques sitting in the tree — no, not sitting, but actually dangling in mid-air. His hands and feet were moving with extraordinary speed, as he spun a bridge from the tree to the window — a complicated web of roses and thorns. "The choice is yours," he said in her mind. "You can stay in the morass or come to me. The bridge I'm spinning has only one lane. It leads from you to me and back. Don't let anyone else touch it. One false step, and we're doomed, we're doomed."

Hanke pulled herself away from the window. She felt like laughing. Her sides were splitting with repressed laughter.

"There's no moon!" she remarked to the jacket hanging on a nail.

Gottlieb responded with a grating laugh. "It can't be," he said. "You must have looked in the wrong direction. Tell me something, Hanke, tell me about yourself. Are you still so devoted to the Spanish revolution?"

"I do what I have to," she said. "When you get well, you'll help out, too — if not with a rifle, then with your pen. Someday your name will be writ large in Yiddish literature."

Gottlieb stretched out a hand and pulled her close.

"It's good to hear such words, even if they are not to be believed. It's good to hold your hand, to look at your blooming face. Thank you, Hanke."

Hanke sat on the edge of the bed, not daring to move. The shade on the night lamp was full of burn holes, which formed two human eyes, a nose and a mouth that yawned open, deep and black. It was Jacques's mouth, hollow and mute. My God, Hanke wept inwardly, why did you give me such a divided soul? Will it ever be whole again? Her shadow on the wall had two heads, one fused into the other. Unintentionally she allowed a stifled sigh to escape her lips.

"God forbid!" Gottlieb cried. "Don't take it to heart. The devil is not as black as he's made out to be. My book of poetry will be published soon. A sanatorium is waiting for me. I promise not to trouble you anymore. This is the crossroads where we part company. I'm going west. You, my dear, are standing in the sun. Stand your ground and don't let the winds of fortune divert you from your path. Forgive me, my dear, I never meant to hurt you. I love you, Hanke. What more can I say? I was prepared to die in your arms. I wanted to swallow the little white pills and fall into an eternal sleep in your arms. It seemed so romantic, so dignified, so heroic — I thought I could fight back and show the Angel of Death who was boss. But when you came, everything changed. Your presence revived me. Bees are buzzing in my blood. Don't tremble, Hanke, true love is gentle. Just one kiss, one and only one."

Hanke didn't resist. She buried her head in the pillow and surrendered her body to his searching hands, his urgent body, his pleading lips.

<hr />

After midnight, Gottlieb fell asleep. Hanke carefully freed herself from his arms and slid off the bed. Gottlieb opened his eyes. He smiled briefly, turned over, and fell back asleep with his eyes and mouth open. His face, gray and gaunt, twitched nervously. She waited for him to close his eyes, but they remained open, as if he was watching her in his sleep.

Hanke stepped backwards to the door, her eyes fixed on him. The area from the bed to the door seemed to go on for miles. Finally she opened the door. The shade on the night light trembled. One last glance — and she closed the door behind her.

She spent the night outdoors. A hidden force drove her from street to street, and she submitted to its power like a sleepwalker with no control over her impulses. By the fence of the Père Lachaise cemetery she sat down on a bench. She lifted her eyes to the heavens teeming with stars. A cool wind crept over her like a fresh bed sheet. She shivered, and the stars in heaven shivered with her. She tried to think but was unable to form a single thought. Tucking her feet under herself, she rolled herself into a ball, as if she were a worm churned up out of the ground by a digging machine, abandoned under the immensity of God's star-studded velvet sky.

THE POWER OF A MELODY

F ar, far away, in the regions of the world encased in ice, there is no marking of time. No seasons, no renewal, no withering away — only a vast, enshrouded realm where frost and snow and primeval winds go unrecorded in any chronology. There, where all paths come to an end, the footsteps of eternity make no imprint in the void.

As a refugee from the green world, I brought my own seasons with me, smuggling them across the border with the songs that lived inside me, each one rooted in its own climate, its own hues and tones, its own purpose. There were songs that flowed with summer rains and apple blossoms, bringing to life the beauty of the Sabbath and the spirit of holidays past. There were songs that gladdened my heart and songs that drove me to the brink of despair. The song of all songs was the one that had brought me to him.

I never knew the date of his death. All I remember is that it was harvest time. Rows of haystacks stretched to the horizon like golden mountains. Hemp was soaking in the river. Carts loaded with the abundance of the field hurried along the back roads toward home. The pair of storks roosting on our roof had just that morning flown off with their young, leaving behind an empty nest.

Sealed railroad cars had taken my parents away, and now I lingered in the doorway, the last to leave the house. Aside from a few flies, no one was about. I took a crust of bread from my pack and spread its crumbs on the table, then opened the window facing the river. Perhaps the flies would eat their fill, then step out for a stroll on God's free earth.

Dressed in peasant clothing, I went into the woods and started up the path toward the place where we had agreed to meet. I did not look back. On one shoulder I carried a wreath of garlic, on the other a head of cabbage. Hidden in my heart I carried the map that would lead us to the Promised Land.

The sun grew warmer. Silver threads of flax floated on the breeze. Certain that no evil could occur on such a blessed day, I felt no fear. I even hummed a melody to myself, a melody of resistance, heroism, and victory. On I walked, singing my song — until I spotted his gray jacket and his red forelock hanging from a tree.

I had nothing with which to dig his grave, and so I hid him under a pile of golden-red leaves. I covered him with branches and sharp, pungent pine needles. I did not stop singing; the melody continued of its own accord. Then I left the green earth behind. I wandered over the steppes, hitched rides in horse-drawn carts and crowded railway cars, travelling across the land known as the Russian bear, until I reached the very center of the frozen heartland.

There, in my cellar home, I adorned the damp walls with summer songs and filled the empty days and nights with remembrance. In the evening when I had devoured my portion of bread and slaked my thirst with hot water, the songs suppressed within me began to sing. Singing, I lowered myself to the floor and peered out of the little barred window that stood level with the setting sun. I sang to the sun that was giving up its light and departing for other worlds.

In those moments my cellar room glowed with the sun's grace. The crimson rays penetrated my barred window, spread out, and split open like the glittering blades of a pair of shears.

Seated in the open jaws of the shears as if in a boat, I swam to the edge of heaven, where the snow burned like the coals in our fireplace back home. Overcome with longing for that cozy warmth, I flung the thin branch of that tree of infamy into the fire and kindled the ebbing melody once more. The flames leapt up, wave after wave, incinerating the white snow and the black pine forest and burying my shears of light under a mountain of ash.

I rose from my seat, shook off the ash, and began pacing back and forth in the dark, searching for a rhythm to match my song. I peered into corners, felt along walls. The creak of an empty drawer reminded me of something. I paused for a moment, pondering, then broke out in a sweat. With trembling fingers, I reached into the drawer and felt around in the emptiness. Palaces of cobwebs exploded under my touch and spiders ran over me like leeches hungry for my blood. Instinctively I raised my right leg for extra leverage as I tried to free my hand. But the cold sweat dripping from my body swelled the planks of wood and drew my arm in deeper and deeper, dragging with it my throat, my neck, my head, my powers of concentration. . . .

I would have screamed for help, but I knew no one would hear me. I'd begun to resign myself to my fate when my fingers closed around a candle, a tallow candle inside the empty drawer.

All fear left me. Effortlessly I pulled my arm out of the drawer. I lit the candle with the spark of my melody. At that moment, I knew that today was the first anniversary of his death. I felt it in the rhythm of my blood. The song that arose within me resounded with the mighty tones of "Hatikvah," the Israeli national anthem. I placed the candle in the window to light the way to where the sun had set.

For a long time, I stood over the candle I'd lit in his memory. It smelled like dough fried with honey, like the hair of my beloved when he would lay his head in my lap and sing our song, the song of promise, the blessed song of good fortune. . . . Above us, the sheltering branches of the plum tree seemed to us like those of a cedar. We paid no mind to the black ravens on the fence. Before our eyes fluttered a swarm of white butterflies, and with our singing we gave life to the song of life.

After the candle had burned out, I saw that the phoenix had arisen from the ashes and was pointing out the road I had lost, a footpath over fire and water. The wolves in the forest had ceased their howling. I took that as a sign that day had broken.

YOSELE

When Tsirele Zilber fell out of the window and died, neither the radio nor the newspapers reported the news. After all, there's no limit to the misfortunes that can befall a person. Every day in New York, people are killed, injured, raped, robbed, and burned. Many speed the end by their own hand.

There was no doubt that Tsirele's death was an accident. No one suspected suicide. Yoyne, her husband, did wonder, but he buried the thought deep within himself, along with all his other suspicions.

Morning in the Zilber household was the most painful time of day. Still unaccustomed to the luxury of their "golden years," the couple slept late — he in his room, she in hers. Yoyne ate his breakfast alone, while Tsirele lay in bed, covers pulled up over her head, and waited for him to go out to buy the newspaper as usual. He enjoyed strolling up the avenue with the paper under his arm, peering into shops, counting the customers. Sometimes he would step into the store that he himself had managed for more than twenty years. There he might buy a carton of milk or a loaf of bread, and if it was a busy day he would gladly help serve the customers.

Tsirele would lie in bed and wait. As soon as the door closed behind Yoyne, she would get out of bed and go to the window to observe his slow, careful stride. An autumnal sadness weighed heavily on his shoulders, as if they sensed the first signs of winter. She didn't mention this to him. To herself, though, she never stopped talking. As much as possible, Tsirele avoided going out, especially when the weather was sunny and fine, a perfect day for women to sit in the park and chat. "Yes, a lovely day, a splendid day, red flowers are in bloom on the black earth . . . " Such a day was good for committing suicide — the thought, long hidden in memory, flashed through her mind, surprising her with its suddenness. As the women talked, Tsirele nodded her head and said whatever slipped off her tongue, no matter how inappropriate or foolish — anything to cover up the relentless intensity surging in her soul night and day — between herself and Yosele. Tsirele considered any interruption of their inner connection to be a sin. She had never forgiven herself for the sin of betraying Yosele's memory by marrying Yoyne and acting as a mother to his daughter. She treated the child well, but she was not, could not be, her mother. Whenever she spoke to her, told her a story, or sang her a little tune, it was always for him, for her Yosele, not for Yoyne's daughter.

"Once there was a Sorele," Tsirele would sing: "A lovely girl was she / and she did have a handsome brother, Yosele was he." When Yoyne was at home, she would replace the name "Yosele" with "Moyshele," the way it appeared in the song. Once, the child herself sang, "She did have a handsome brother, Yosele was he," and Yoyne glanced sideways at his wife and saw how the knife shook in her hand.

Yoyne knew that Tsirele never stopped thinking about her Yosele. Her nightmares made their mornings difficult. A strained silence hung between them, as if a reproving finger were pointing at each of them in turn. Yoyne knew that she wasn't asleep when she lay in bed with the blankets pulled up over her head. She knew that he knew and was pretending not to know. He knew that when she talked about curtains she was talking not about covering the windows but rather about the ghosts that tormented her. She knew that he knew — but she couldn't help herself. Yosele had been and still was the reason for her existence. She stayed alive so that he could live, with her, through her — so that he could be with her through thick and thin, taking part in all her experiences, so that she could keep his memory alive in her sealed universe, in her private temple behind her home-made sacred curtain.

When Yoyne had first met Tsirele, she had been feverish, calling out in delirium, warning Yosele not to go into the village. When her fever subsided, she could not recognize anyone. She insisted that her name was Katerina, that she hailed from the village of Khlopufke, that she had a husband and a son named Yosip there. Yoyne tried to remind her that the two of them had gone to school together, that he had known her father, the wealthy timber merchant, as well as her husband the dentist, whom the Germans had shot immediately upon their arrival. And there, in the empty ruins, they'd become husband and wife.

Yoyne brought his eight-year-old daughter as a dowry to the match. Both of them lit memorial candles, not on the day their loved ones had actually perished, but on the day they'd been parted from them forever.

For Yoyne, that day was the eve of Passover, when his young wife, with their nursing baby in her arms, had been sent to the right line, and he with their little girl to the left. The warm sunshine and the mild breeze smelling of spring had caressed the assembled Jews.

Within the crowd was an outsider who had escaped from a distant region. He told of massacres that had killed an entire city of Jews in a matter of hours. People looked at his tattered clothing and unshaven face and paid him no mind. Surely he must be a lunatic, they thought, for who would kill an entire city full of Jews, men, women, and children? At worst, they were being taken away to do hard labor. Whatever else the Germans might be, they were surely a civilized people. Only a madman could think up such a horror. . . . So they stood and milled about, waiting, and then, lo and behold, there he was, the commandant, tall and slender, wearing black glasses and white gloves. He stood by the door of his cargo truck giving orders: "To the right, to the left!" Yoyne's wife, with the baby in her arms, waved to him. He waved back. She smiled, he smiled. . . .

These days Yoyne thought about how naïve he'd been. And perhaps he was still naïve? He looked at the German neighbor with whom he exchanged a daily greeting, searching for a trace of the knife-sharp chin and ice-cold eyes that did not blink when children sobbed and pleaded for mercy. This one looked him straight in the eye, smiling politely. Yoyne searched for the mark of Cain hidden behind the polite smile, and although he didn't find it, he couldn't bring himself to return the smile. After each encounter with the neighbor, a melancholy overtook him. At night he lay in bed wrestling with the question of what could turn a person into a murder-machine. He wondered whether he himself could ever be part of such a mass psychosis. Would he be able to split open the head of his neighbor's only son merely because he was German? Would he be able to watch his neighbor's house burn down and not run to the rescue? Could he set it on fire himself and watch to see how his neighbor reacted? These macabre thoughts kept him wide awake until he swallowed a pill that would transport him from nightmarish reality to nightmarish dream.

First thing every morning, Yoyne hurried to buy the Yiddish newspaper as well as the *Times*. Perhaps they would explain to him the riddle of man. Perhaps.

Indeed, it was with the newspaper under his arm that Yoyne arrived to find the ambulance parked in front of his house. Tsirele lay on the ground with a fractured skull, her hair disheveled, a crowd surrounding her. The German neighbor and his two children were there, standing and staring. Should Yoyne throw himself at him and strangle him with his bare hands? The thought lasted only a second. The police opened the door. They looked for evidence of an intruder but found none. Money, jewelry, the wedding ring from her first husband — all were untouched. The beds were made, the carpet freshly vacuumed and free of footprints.

The corpse was brought to burial. Yoyne's daughter wailed as he recited the mourner's prayer. In the evening he lit a memorial candle. The flame blazed up, throwing trembling shadows on the wall. Yoyne's lips also trembled, but no sound emerged.

Time passed in its usual way. People forgot, but the birds remembered. The only witnesses to her fatal fall, they continued to arrive, filling the courtyard with their hungry calls as they waited for the window to open, a head to appear, a hand to shower them with grain. They waited for her just as she had once waited for them. Tsirele had also fed peanuts to the squirrels. Every nut she tossed helped her repay an old debt promised to their cousins in the far-off Polish forest.

How happy her Yosele had been when he managed to dig up a few soft nuts from their hiding place. He had tracked them on all fours like a strange little wild animal with red hair. How proud he had been when he mastered the art of climbing trees. Once he found a tail shed from the carcass of a fox. He fastened it to his trousers, feeling that in so doing he had attained the status of a beast that could move freely on God's earth. His gift for seeking and finding ways to make their life easier was limitless, while Tsirele felt utterly inept. Before the war, she never knew where her daily bread had come from. Now, in the forest, she was completely dependent on the little boy with the wild tail, who surveyed their surroundings from the treetop and determined when it was safe to sneak over to the woman in the village, a wet nurse from whom he could beg a few eggs and a crust of bread to keep them both alive.

For a long time, mother and son had hidden at the home of the nurse, who was also hiding their possessions. Then neighbors began to notice that she seemed loaded with money, always carrying food parcels that cost a small fortune. Rumors spread that something not quite right was taking place under her roof. It was then that she showed them the cave in the forest where her grandfather had lived for many years after murdering a customs officer and escaping from prison.

Every time Yosele returned safely with something to eat, mother and son celebrated as if at a feast. Afterwards, Yosele would lay his head in her lap and Tsirele would stroke his hair and hunt for the lice that were devouring him. They called the vermin "Germans" and considered each murdered German a personal triumph.

Such was the reality of that time — a time that had lost all sense of time, of yesterday, of tomorrow. All that remained was the now, the moment, the instant of beholding, of feeling the other's warmth and devotion. Sometimes it seemed to her that she and Yosele were the last survivors left in the world into which she had been born and raised to live out her life. She imagined emerging from the cave and discovering that the sky was no longer the sky, that the sun would not move from its allotted spot, that the mountains had sunk. The face of the earth would be covered in trees, or perhaps the sea would have overflowed and drowned the land, leaving the whale lying on the naked sand, staring with blank eyes at the extinguished sun. . . .

For Yosele, she painted other pictures. They would stay in the forest, living on fish from the river, berries from the earth, milk from the deer, honey from the bees. She would season their food with herbs that would make him big and strong. Then they would leave the forest and go looking for a bride for him, a bride blessed with the charm of spring flowers. They would bring children into the world, decent and upstanding children.

The last day Tsirele saw her Yosele was a Sunday. This she knew from the tolling of the church bells. For several days she had been burning with fever. The sound of the bells hypnotized her, seeming to lift her out of the grave and lay her before the throne of God. All her cares fell away as she reclined at the feet of the Creator. The light that enveloped Him embraced her. All was well, well, well . . .

When she awakened, her fever had subsided. She had no idea how long she had been sleeping. Was it still the same day? She realized she was alone. Yosele was not in the cave. He must have been frightened by her appearance and run to the nurse for help. Tsirele tried to stand, fell back, then crawled to the mouth of the cave and stuck out her head. A new-fallen snow was already melting in the spring sun. The snow was smooth and undisturbed, with no sign of Yosele's footprints. Perhaps he had stayed overnight at the nurse's house? She knew she was fooling herself — Yosele would never do such a thing. He had gone to fetch her some milk. She remembered trying to prevent him from going. Perhaps she had not tried hard enough? The tolling of the bells stifled her thoughts and stilled her hands. Her tongue, as if paralyzed, emitted no sound. Perhaps she'd wanted him to go so that he could bring back a taste of milk to moisten her lips? Tsirele touched her face to the snow, drawing its cool fluidity into herself. Her tongue loosened. "Yosele!" she called out with wild desperation, and heard her echo answering: Yo-se-lehhh. . . .

Whenever snow fell, Tsirele would light a memorial candle. Not wanting to upset Yoyne, she lit it in silence, inside her heart. The flame extended all the way to the distant forest. The trees were alight like candles, rays of sunlit gold that melted, dripping wax like white lambs, frightened lambs without a shepherd that ran helter-skelter into the night. The nightingale sang. The frogs croaked. Needing fresh air, Tsirele opened the window. The birds were waiting. They, too, would risk their lives for a mouthful of bread. A fat tomcat lurked nearby. On the telephone wire, some birds kept watch while those on the ground pecked at the grain. Perhaps the birds on the wire were the mothers? She, the mother of her only child, had lain like a stone and allowed her child to run into the fire. Tsirele threw out a handful of seeds. She talked to herself without stopping. Sometimes she spoke to the birds, not caring whether they heard or understood. She spoke because she had to speak. She even told them about her two miscarriages. She had not been able to disgrace Yosele's memory by allowing another being to take root in the place where he had begun.

Tsirele spoke as the birds pecked. When those on the wire became greedy for a bite and descended to the perilous ground, Tsirele took over the vigil for them. She knew that the gluttonous tomcat was crouching in the bushes. He was not even hungry; he was simply luxuriating in his good fortune. The collar at his throat was set with colored stones. He did not eat the birds. He bit their necks in two and looked on with pleasure until they stopped moving.

To Yoyne and his daughter she did not speak about Yosele. They who had not looked into his eyes, who had not felt his trembling pulse or rejoiced in his triumphs, who had not shared in his fear, could not understand what he meant to her. She spoke instead to the birds above, to the squirrels on the ground, to the wind in the air. She heard her own echo as it resounded across the courtyard: "Yosele! Yosele?"

Her husband's daughter was preparing a bar mitzvah celebration for her son. Of course Tsirele would go to the party dressed in her best, as befitted a mother-in-law. Perhaps she would also dance. Why shouldn't she? After all, she had lived to see the Brown Shirts defeated. She had a roof over her head, shoes on her feet, a dress on her body, a husband — and yet all the blessings in the world could not restore Yosele's unlived life or the life of the generations he was destined to bring to the world. From whom could she demand her due? To whom could she submit her claim? Common sense dictated that she admit defeat, but her heart could not accept the verdict.

Whenever a holiday arrived, Tsirele went looking for Holocaust literature to read, the memorial volumes of the annihilated Jewish towns. She did this not to dampen the holiday cheer, but because she couldn't do otherwise, dared not do otherwise. Her conscience compelled her not only to obey God's commands but — more difficult yet — to strive to be the master of her own destiny.

On the Sunday morning a week before Passover, wet snow filled the air and covered the ground like a white tablecloth. Tsirele stood by the open window tossing seeds for the birds. Her thoughts wandered over the pathways of her life. Images raced before her eyes. She saw her Yosele running on all fours, the fox tail tangled between his legs. The footprints he had left behind looked like those of a little animal. Tsirele shook the remains of the seeds from the paper bag. Suddenly she spotted the brown tomcat springing from his hiding place. "Yosele!" she called out in an otherworldly voice. She leaned out of the window a bit too far. Her body gave way. Yosele was saved — Tsirele Zilber lay in the wet snow, her skull split, her mouth open, as if she were still calling: "Yosele! Yosele?"

THE BAG LADY OF
SEVENTH AVENUE

She sat on the cement floor, an island in the turbulent whirlwind swirling around Penn Station in New York. The commotion did not affect her. Protected within her private isolation, she sat apart on her little rubber cushion. A plastic bag stuffed with raggedy clothes stood open at her feet. Among the rags were scattered quarters, nickels, pennies. The change stuck to wads of chewing gum, orange peels, crusts of bread, chocolate, cigarette butts.

Detached amid the tumultuous sea, the bag lady did not react to the gifts of passersby; she accepted the quarters, the pennies, the orange peels with the same apathetic facial expression that she had adopted once and since then never changed.

Under her broad hat, her face was invisible. Even so she kept her head lowered. She wore the same outfit in summer and winter: a sweater on top of a sweater, a worn-out cape, baggy black pants, slippers without socks. From beneath her hat, her unkempt black hair half revealed and half concealed long earrings that glittered like a snowstorm on the surface of the sea.

I don't know when or why I became accustomed to tossing a coin into her basket. Over time, as I commuted on the Long Island Rail Road, the habit became a matter of personal necessity. I felt upset if I had no coin to toss into her bag as I raced to catch the train.

I never stopped to strike up a conversation with her, because I believed then and still believe that it's insulting to speak to another person while looking down from above. Nor did I have the courage to sit down next to her on the bare floor.

Once I did encounter her face-to-face in the women's restroom, the one inside Penn Station. It was a stormy afternoon. An early December snow mixed with rain, sharp as glass, had wrested her from her seat and driven her into the luxurious realm of female urine and perfume.

She was sitting in a corner by the wall, her possessions at her feet. I noticed that her cape had a new tear in the right sleeve. I approached her and seated myself cozily on the bench beside her. After a long moment of tense silence, I asked if she would like to exchange her cape for a warm winter coat, the one my late mother had left me. I assured her it would fit; she looked to be my mother's exact size.

She lowered her head as usual so that her earrings touched her shoulders and answered in a voice that sounded intimate and familiar — yet strange coming from her mouth. "No, no!" she said, as if speaking to her slippers, not to me. "This cape is good enough for me, and I'm never letting go of it. It's been with me through thick and thin and I'm going to keep it until I die."

I looked into the mirror and saw that she was looking at me with the same stealthy curiosity with which I was looking at her.

I can't say I saw the bag lady, or even thought about her, every day. But whenever her image flitted into my imagination, I found myself thinking of bizarre gifts for her: feathers from the bird that hides its head in the sand, bouquets of desert flowers, and miniature seashells, each shell a tower reaching for the heavens. I adorned her hat with the flowers. Around her neck, I hung beads of blood-red coral, the kind that trace their lineage to the bottom of the sea. I conjured for her a honey cake like the one my mother used to make, a strudel flavored with Jewish spices. In my mind, I tossed these gifts to the bag lady, but only when her eyes were closed. I imagined that if she opened her eyes, she'd think I was an angel from the other world.

This was what I imagined doing, but I didn't pursue the fantasy any further. Days, months went by and still she sat in the same place, wearing the same clothes summer and winter, as if blessed with an internal temperature unaffected by the weather. So engraved was she in my thoughts that I expected to see her at her post no matter the hour of day or night, like the lions standing guard at the Public Library.

On the day my course ended and summer vacation began, I decided the time had come to present her with a gift. With this in mind, I arrived at the corner of 34th Street and Seventh Avenue. A famous rock band happened to be giving a concert that day. Penn Station was flooded with young people. The concert was completely sold out, and a kind of black market had sprung up. Tickets were going for outrageous prices. Police on horseback surrounded the enormous crowd of excited fans. I could barely push my way toward the entrance to the Long Island Rail Road. Suddenly an ambulance sped onto the scene and paramedics blocked my path. I stopped in my tracks and craned my neck to see who was injured. Then I started to tremble. Word spread that someone had been thrown down the stairs. Right away I had a feeling it was the bag lady. Then I spotted her on the stretcher, covered with blood and scratches. Her hat lay on the ground and her disheveled hair covered her eyes and face. I grabbed her hat and her seven bags and got into the ambulance with her. The paramedic unbuttoned her sweaters, baring her bosom. Engraved on the medallion nestled between her breasts was her name: Rosa Shapiro-Scott.

The name Shapiro burned into me. Shapiro was my mother's maiden name. I tried to convince myself it was just a coincidence. Shapiro was a popular name. Why go off on a wild goose chase?

After the eventful day, my sleep was a muddle of nightmares. I eluded one danger only to fall prey to another. Police on horseback pursued me. Bats tangled themselves in my hair. And she, the bag lady with the seven packages, pointed bloody fingers at me, "She, she's the culprit!"

I woke, then fell back to sleep. This time my mother appeared before me and stood at the door, not daring to cross the threshold. Knowing that I was afraid of her blue face, the glass shards on her eyes, her white shrouds, she turned away. "Stay with me, mama!" I screamed without sound. Only at dawn, awakened by the summer birds nesting in my tree, did I leave these bad dreams behind.

The summer flew by more quickly than I would have liked, and I thought no more of Rosa Shapiro-Scott. Before returning to work, I made my annual visit to my parents' graves. I took along a small spade for digging up the weeds and a pair of shears for trimming the azalea shrubs. Before I began, I stopped to look at the gravestone that united my parents in death as they had been in life. As I stood, contemplating everything and nothing, I noticed that the free plot of land on my mother's side had been taken. I took out my glasses and peered curiously at the engraved letters: Mrs. Rosa Shapiro-Scott, daughter of R. Shiele and Shifre Shapiro . . .

I read no further. Leaning my head against my mother's gravestone, I stood and waited for answers, although I knew full well that my questions must die stillborn, sealed away for eternity.

Under the naked sky, the summer birds hurried to other horizons. Usually I don't watch them fly away. I simply look forward with pleasure to their return. But now I looked after the long, fluttering rows and felt that they were taking something of mine with them — something as secret and mysterious as the force that drove them to and fro.

En Route to Divorce

Phyllis Tidewater boarded an airplane bound for Reno, Nevada, and settled into her window seat. She put away her purse and raincoat and took off her gloves, then leaned her head against the pane and closed her eyes. She tried to quiet her nerves, but the tension would not let up. She reached for a magazine and began leafing through it backwards from the last page, the way she liked to, but to no avail — her thoughts flew over the words like an eraser, obliterating one after the other. Once again she rested her head against the window. She watched as the plane lifted off the tarmac and ascended above the lines on the runway, higher and higher over the fog cover into a world of sheer oblivion, a world untouched by human hands, unchanged since the six days of creation. A golden sun rose within her tiny window frame, vanished, then reappeared. All around stretched a blue transparent void. The earth below was invisible, covered by a white-gray expanse that trembled like a meringue.

Phyllis gazed out at the primeval spectacle. The emptiness cast her into a state of atavistic terror. Here was a world without time, without change, without death. There was no I, no you — no sign pointing the way from A to B. Phyllis recoiled from the wild desolation. Sensing danger, her inner self gravitated to the familiar, the personal, the clearly delineated path she was following to wherever it might lead. She'd thought everything through thousands of times already. There was nothing more to consider. All the formalities were taken care of, except for her signature. As soon as she signed her name, she would become a free woman.

This, in any event, was what Phyllis Tidewater had been thinking on the day she left her house alone, without her husband, for the very first time. She had slammed the door, but these days a slammed door no longer raised eyebrows. Times had changed. In the twentieth century, women's rights had finally arrived. Old values were burned on new altars. Women threw their engagement rings onto the open fire, and the word "freedom" was in the air, stoking the fantasy of liberty in every sphere, including sex.

Here on the airplane, between heaven and earth, Phyllis wondered what had become of Nora after she walked out on her husband and slammed the door in Ibsen's play, *A Doll's House*. Did other doors open for her? Did she stand outside frightened and despairing, wondering where to turn? Did she carry the banner of "freedom" all over the world? In the uncharted depths did she bump up against a boundary or a fence marked "danger"? Perhaps she got drunk in singles bars, whiled away the nights in discotheques, went to bed with someone different every night.

Every birth has its pangs, Phyllis told herself, although in fact her mother had not suffered from such pains. If her mother liked a young man she didn't hesitate to drop her handkerchief. This was the ploy she'd used on Phyllis's father one Sunday afternoon as she strolled slowly down Fifth Avenue, keeping one eye on the shop windows and the other on the youthful passersby. A young man in front of her was wearing a straw hat, a brightly colored jacket, polished shoes. He walked with measured steps, head high and shoulders erect, quite unlike the tailors from the East Side, and his outfit reminded her of a flower garden. Without a moment's misgiving, she ran ahead and dropped her handkerchief. "If he picks it up and gives it back," she thought, "then he's a gentleman. If he doesn't, he's not worth my time."

Father did pick up the handkerchief, which was made of pure silk and hand-embroidered with girlish dreams, redolent of the spells and incantations of great-great-grandmothers and smelling of French perfume. And although the two of them knew they were neighbors on the East Side, the magic of the handkerchief worked a special charm.

As for Phyllis, she carried no handkerchief, nor would any respectable man stoop to retrieve the scrap of tissue paper that had taken the place of the hand-embroidered square perfumed with dreams. That romantic era was long gone. Perhaps even in her mother's day the handkerchief trick was out of date. For that matter, maybe divorce itself was no longer new. Possibly the so-called trendsetters, the founders of the movement, had slipped away, leaving their followers in God's hands. Jerry Rubin was on Wall Street, and word was that the loud-mouthed girl with the face half-obscured by glasses had found herself a mistress; the two of them were writing a book about the feminist mystique that would surely earn them a fortune.

Phyllis looked out the window and thought of the eagle wings that were carrying her upwards and dangling her over the abyss. It was a world without doors, without locks, fences, or borders. Like Noah's dove, her eye sought a resting place, a twig upon which to land, a moral principle to guide her way — in vain. The blue wilderness — desolate and empty — remained mute. She could pull the shade down over the window, buy a pair of earphones, and muffle her thoughts with the lives of the heroes gallivanting on the screen. Or she could have a good cry, washing away her despair with a few salty tears. If a bride could cry at her wedding, she could cry over her divorce.

The wide-bellied plane was half empty. Across the aisle sat two young men whom Phyllis had noticed in the boarding area. Paradoxically, even in her current frame of mind, she still had an eye for a certain sexy look. She'd even noted the leather attaché cases they were carrying, the suede shoes with pointed toes that stepped so softly over the plush carpet. The one who'd stood in line with her had long hair and a Van Dyke beard. She hadn't seen the other man's face and didn't dare take a look for fear that people would notice her and somehow figure out that she was on her way to a divorce.

In the narrow aisle, on the way to their seats, the bearded man had stepped aside to let her go ahead. He'd said something she hadn't quite caught. Instead of answering, she'd shrewdly tossed her carefully coiffed auburn hair so that it parted like a theater curtain to reveal her face.

Now the bearded man appeared again. He had moved to a new seat with his attaché case under one arm and a cocktail in the other. His glance, which had so casually brushed over her before, now seared into her. In the dark realm of her soul, glowing wings began to flutter in a wild dance. The sun, which had been flitting from one side of the plane to the other, was now fixed at her window. The tears she had been holding back sprang out from behind her long eyelashes and smeared her mascara. The magnetic needle that measured her heartbeat quivered out of control. There he was! The one she'd been waiting for! His briefcase was stuffed with poetry, love poems, music, perhaps even an entire symphony.

Phyllis Tidewater covered her face. Why now? she asked herself. Why not yesterday or a year ago? Why do I have such bad luck? Why do these opportunities come along when I'm least prepared? If I weren't in such a desperate state, I would go to the washroom, freshen my hair and make-up and pull open my sweater. "Look," I'd announce, "I'm free! I've tossed my bra onto the bonfire and I'm getting a divorce!"

Since Phyllis had left her husband and become a free woman, she had taken to laughing at herself. But unlike tears, which brought her some measure of relief, the laughter hit her hard. There was no happy medium. No sooner had she ascended into the sublime than she would plunge into the darkest depths.

The blond stewardess who had been walking up and down the aisle had now taken a seat beside the bearded man. Phyllis could hear her laughter, then his. She envied the stewardess, who took life so lightly — and death too, no doubt, or she would not be a stewardess. Maybe she was trying to escape the earth itself with all its problems. Phyllis Tidewater strained to hear what they were laughing about. But something in her wept. She wept with dry eyes. She wept for all the passing meteors that flared up only to dwindle into nothingness. The man with the attaché case who was now romancing the stewardess would soon disappear. The stewardess knew; she was used to serving as a transit station. Maybe the two of them were making plans to meet somewhere more intimate. The blond stewardess was not constrained by harsh "Thou shalt not's." She pressured the bearded man and didn't let up. If she weren't manipulating him so, he would be sitting here, with Phyllis. She knew it; she felt it. His gaze alighted on her like a bird entering the nest and beginning to sing. In her mind she joined in: "Yes, the trip is fine, the view fantastic. No, I'm not traveling on business — I'm off to a wedding! Yes, people still get married." She would introduce herself as Linda Levin, which would make clear that she was Jewish and compel him to introduce himself too. She knew how to tell who was a family man and who was single. If he turned out to be Jewish, without ties to wife or child, she would show her cards and the two of them would share a good laugh. But if he stammered, offering only his work number instead of his home address, she would give him a false number — that of a friend she'd briefly roomed with. If he tried to find her, well, good luck to him and good luck to her friend.

For her ex-roommate, sex was an act of revenge, a way of getting back at the parents who had kept her under lock and key after she had an abortion at sixteen. Her sexual excesses had driven Phyllis out of the apartment. They'd had separate bedrooms, but Phyllis could still hear every rustle through the wall. The nights were a torment for her, sleepless and erotically charged. The music that accompanied the pair's exertions thrummed in her blood like the buzzing of wild bees, leaving behind a taste of bitter honey.

Now Phyllis lived alone. When she came home from work in the evenings she did not unlock her door right away. Instead she rang the doorbell a few times — a trick to give any intruders time to escape. Her fear of criminals came to obsess her to the point that she looked upon every date as a potential pervert, if not an actual murderer.

The first party Phyllis attended as a single woman stripped her of all illusions. The acquaintance of an acquaintance who had invited her disappeared as soon as they arrived, leaving Phyllis alone in the doorway with no one to turn to. She immediately forgot what she'd been told to do: to mingle so she'd look like an experienced partygoer, and not to tell anyone she was separated. The men attending these parties, the acquaintance said, were not looking for a serious relationship. The rare couple who actually fell in love was truly a miracle.

Phyllis stood and stared at the scene. Black lights adorned with red ribbons blazed in all four corners of the hall and the stereo was on at full blast. People were dancing, not in pairs but alone. A Venus in jeans with bare breasts and hair bleached gold danced opposite a young man in a petticoat. Newly schooled in feminism, Phyllis didn't know if she should take this as a symbol of self-expression or a step back into the jungle. Middle-aged men with martinis wandered from group to group, searching for new acquaintances, or more precisely, new victims on whom they could lavish their corrupt attentions.

Phyllis stayed by the door. No one greeted her or asked who she was or who had brought her. Finally, a red-faced young man wearing what appeared to be a cape on his shoulders offered her a glass of red wine. The glass shook in his hand and spilled on her white dress.

A passerby burst out laughing. "Announcing a red letter day?" he guffawed.

Phyllis summoned her courage and went to find a bathroom where she could wash out the stain. Certain rooms were closed, she noticed, apparently locked from the inside. On the outside, signs with giant letters proclaimed that the rooms were in use.

A woman in men's clothing took her by the arm with a friendly smile and ushered her into the bathroom. She bolted the door and helped Phyllis take off her dress, then ripped off her underwear. "Not bad," she sniffed. "You're a big girl now, so what's the harm in — " The more Phyllis struggled, the more aggressive the woman became. Finally Phyllis tore open the door. Half naked, clutching her dress, she ran out into the corridor. "Who invited this bitch?" the woman shouted. She threw Phyllis's underwear after her. "Get out of my house and don't come back!"

"One bad experience isn't the end of the world," Phyllis's acquaintance argued later. "There's a rotten apple in every barrel. New York is so big — there's something for everyone. All you have to do is choose."

What exactly was choice? Phyllis wondered bitterly. Could you walk into a store or open a catalog and pick out a life based on what you saw on the page? Let's say the young man with the briefcase appeals to me. What would happen if I went over to him: "Excuse me, sir," I'd say, "I'm very attracted to you. You belong in a picture I dreamed up by the light of the moon. I've been searching heaven and earth for you. I long to rest my head on your shoulder, to feel your caress and hear your voice. I see us sipping champagne together under waving palm trees, surrounded by brown-skinned hula-hula girls adorned with wreaths and crowns who swivel their hips in time with the waves. And the sun, ah, the sun — see how it flies from one window to the next!"

Phyllis pulled down the shade. She no longer wanted to see the cosmic desert. She went to the restroom and stood for a long time before the mirror. She brushed her hair, applied lipstick. The burden of maintaining her youth weighed heavily upon her. With a bit more paint on her cheeks, perhaps she could fool the pitiless clock. The "lib" movement was well and good, but in the end a woman was still a woman. She had worked hard to master all the time-tested techniques that flatter a man's machismo. Once she felt sure of her abilities, she realized she was a free woman. She hid her face behind an aggressive mask — and demanded a divorce.

Phyllis looked into the mirror without seeing. She played out the scenes in her head, imagining herself bowing to the dictates of the times and opening her arms to casual passersby. Like two ships in the night, they would get acquainted, then part without reproach or regret.

The parting of ways between Phyllis and her husband had also taken place without regret. She had gone into his arms as if into a fortress — and left as if from a prison. By the time they separated she had actually become allergic to him, complete with headaches, a nervous stomach, and a fiery rash on her face. She couldn't bear his odor or his cold, wet lips. Even his walk irritated her. One side of his body seemed to go forward and the other backward, as if he were dragging some kind of wagon or cart. His blind faith in rules and regulations made him a slave to his own rigid principles.

Phyllis returned to her seat. Within moments, the plane had landed in Denver and the young men with the briefcases were standing up and facing the exit. The blond stewardess was with them. Suddenly, as if remembering something, both men turned their heads and blew Phyllis a good-bye kiss.

Like so many others, Phyllis thought, like so many others. They came and they went. She was finished with that roulette wheel. She didn't want to see who was waiting for them out there in their world. Nor, as the plane continued on to Reno, Nevada, did she want to look down into the desolate abyss.

THE LITTLE RED UMBRELLA

On the day Janet Silver had chosen for the date with the poet she didn't know, it rained. They were supposed to meet in front of a French restaurant. She'd told him he would recognize her by the little red umbrella she'd be carrying regardless of the weather. But he already knew who she was, he said. She'd caught his eye at a Hanukkah party and had made an indelible impression on him. He had a strong intuition that something intangible connected them and had a feeling that a face-to-face meeting would solve the mystery of what it was.

His tone of voice on the telephone did not quite match his words, as if he were reciting a prepared text. He asked no questions. In contrast to other arranged, so-called blind dates, he didn't barrage her with inquiries as to how old she was or what she thought about free love. Typically, the candidates wanted to find out on the spot whether it would be worth their while to spend an evening with her. Janet Silver knew all about them. Her standard response was that she didn't conduct business over the telephone.

The prospect of going out with a poet both frightened and excited her. Years ago, when she'd dreamed of poets, she ended up meeting revolutionaries, for whom poetry smacked of the *petite bourgeoisie*, if not outright treason. She recalled going to hear T.S. Eliot by herself, without either female or male companions. When she entered the auditorium, all the seats were already taken. Standing room was also limited. Someone stepped on the foot she had recently sprained. The wound appeared to be bleeding, but removing the shoe was not an option. People were packed together so tightly that she was barely able to free herself from the curious hand groping under her coat. The tension in the auditorium was overpowering. When the poet finally stood up and began to read, something in her tore. Over the heads of the audience, the gaunt creator of "The Waste Land" reached her and transformed her into a kind of exotic wild animal, from whose depths emerged a hysterical scream followed by a harsh hiccup. After that incident, she stopped attending poetry readings. The shame of being led from the auditorium stayed with her for many years.

Janet now thought that had it not been for that incident, she herself might have written poetry. Instead of writing, she married, raised children, and then lived alone — one more widow on the flooded market. Dilettantes did happen by to share the double bed. They came and went like stars in the night: a washed-up actor, a sock manufacturer, a card player, a man who had left his wife and child to travel around the world in disguise.

The rendezvous with the poet came like a jolt from the very heart of life, awakening the butterflies from their lethargic dozing. White silk wings hovered in the air. The studio apartment, which a moment before had been cold and dark, brightened with an ethereal light. The walls began to sing again. "There's still life at close to fifty," she said to the fly that was spending the winter in her house. Janet did what she could to keep the fly alive. She left bread crumbs for it on the table, an unwashed plate, a drop of water, a bit of sugar. The fly flew from room to room and warmed itself in the sun and, during long winter nights, on the shade of her night light. Once when it was flying around happily, it met another fly just like itself looking out from the mirror in the corridor. It came closer. With its multi-colored antennae it tapped the glass. The fly stayed there for an entire day without moving. It sniffed, licked, spoke and asked the lonely fly to come to it. It stayed like this for an entire day and night until both died.

Once more the walls fell silent. Janet sat from dawn until dusk. Just before sunset her studio came alive. Fantastic patterns streamed through the cracks in the Venetian blinds. Lost ships swam to her mountain, bringing regards from distant lands, magic keys to locked doors. Janet loved to play make-believe; she tried out the keys to the rusty cabins. On each door — a name, each one world-renowned: Churchill gleaming in gold on a black marble sign, Prince and Princess Radziwill, Jean-Paul Sartre and Mme. de Beauvoir. Janet lost her way among the turbines. Madame Butterfly's heartrending song drew her forward. Only Maria Callas could sing so well. She followed the voice through the dark corridors until she reached a door locked from the inside. There was a transom up above. Janet found a chair, climbed up, and peered in. A purple light filled the room. On a bed of sky-blue silk, the Greek was lounging with a high-born lady.

Janet pulled herself back to reality. The room grew dark. The music flickered. As the great Thomas Carlyle once said, "All tomorrows become yesterdays." She accepted the idea without sadness, closed her eyes, and swam away with the phantom ship waiting for her in the harbor.

She swims without moving over still water, not forward but backward in time from today to yesterday, to last year, to what once was. The ship takes her back from the twentieth century to the Middle Ages, to another world, on another continent, to when Galileo proclaimed: "And yet it moves." She leaves him standing up to his neck in water and continues on to the land of Socrates, Plato, and Aristotle, then to the promised land of milk and honey. Moses descends from Mt. Sinai, his head wreathed in burning thorns, bringing the Ten Commandments to the waiting world. The golden calf comes to greet him. The ship swims deeper into primeval times. It passes the well where Rebecca waters her sheep, Abraham smashes the stone idols, and Sarah drives Hagar from her home.

All around is pitch black, but the ship sends out a beam of light that casts a glow over all that is, was, and will be. The farther she goes, the narrower the channel becomes. It leads her into a tight passageway from which she can't extricate herself. The shorelines close in, seizing her in their grip like a pair of shears. The walls burst. The mast collapses. The great heat intensifies. Giant trees grow on the mountains on both sides. Fantastical birds nest in their branches. They fan with their wings, cooling the air. Under an outspread fig tree, Adam dozes. He has just emerged from the soil of the earth, from the salt of the sea, from stardust. He does not yet know the difference between good and evil, life and death, man and woman.

She leaves the ship behind and approaches him. She bends down, far down into the grass. "I'm looking for my little red umbrella," she whispers into his ear. "Without the umbrella the poet will never recognize me." Adam opens his eyes — two bloodshot slits. He blinks and scrapes the weeds from his body. In the glow of the morning star she sees that he is naked, without a fig leaf. She too is naked and unashamed. He extends a hand, and his touch sends feverish tremors over her body, penetrating to the core of her being like the very essence of life that has a will of its own. The heat is tremendous. The snake in the tree is laughing. It laughs loudly, harshly. No, it's not the snake. It's actually the telephone.

Janet Silver pulled herself out of the primeval encounter. It was the poet again. Yes, she remembered that they had an appointment; they were to meet in a French restaurant. But no, she'd made a mistake. The caller was actually an English speaker asking for someone she didn't know. She told him he had the wrong number. "No, I don't, sweetheart," he laughed. "Don't worry, I've got the right number. All I need is your address . . . " Janet hung up on him, but he called back again and again, obscenities streaming from his mouth.

Janet turned on the lights, but her terror did not abate. The telephone continued to ring. She didn't answer. The clock on the nightstand showed that it was just nine-thirty. In an hour's time she'd traveled around the world. If not for the psychopath on the telephone, she could still be dreaming. The red umbrella, the one she'd asked Adam about in the Garden of Eden, came to mind again. Her grandmother had given her the little umbrella when she became a bat mitzvah. It was meant to serve as a magic charm. But she'd put it aside in a corner and forgotten about it. Years went by. Janet never thought about the little umbrella, never remembered it. Only when the poet called did she unthinkingly say he would recognize her by her little red umbrella, regardless of the weather. Now, given her dream, she thought the little red umbrella must be a Freudian symbol. How long would the dream last? she wondered. There was a time when she was content to be independent, free to do whatever she pleased. Now freedom had another meaning. Now it meant she was free to bang her head against the wall and not even hear an echo. And yet she kept searching. She searched, found, lost, and searched again. The search had become a kind of addiction, the shot of alcohol a drunk couldn't do without.

On the night before the date, Janet could not sleep. Her hairpins poked her head like pins in a cushion. Bits of conversation that might arise in the company of a poet jumbled together in her mind. Words that had previously seemed extraordinarily interesting now sounded banal. And the dress she'd selected for the date appeared vulgar in the dark.

At daybreak she fell asleep. As usual, she slept through the time she'd planned to get up. She had no time to bathe or freshen up. She grabbed the first good dress, removed the hairpins, applied some rouge and lipstick, picked up the little red umbrella and left the house.

Outside, a March rain poured down. The passing taxis would not stop. Janet was running in high heels, the little red umbrella high over her head, when suddenly a gust of wind turned the umbrella inside out and ruined her swept-up hairdo. Her face also took a beating: the mascara ran, leaving black streaks. Janet kept running, even while thinking it might be better not to show up for a first date in such a state. The weather forecaster had specifically promised a sunny day, and here was such a flood. To make things worse, the coffeehouses were also overflowing. There was nowhere to hide. She ran on, the little broken umbrella under her arm. Suddenly she felt a hand on her shoulder. Someone held an umbrella over her head. She didn't see his face, but she recognized his voice.

"Where is your little red umbrella?" he asked. Without waiting for a reply, he pulled her toward him. "I thought the rain might keep you away."

They passed the French restaurant, but they didn't stop. The conversation she'd prepared was no longer relevant. She was shocked by his appearance. Not the slightest resemblance to the picture she'd created in her imagination. A Hasidic beard. A broad-brimmed hat. A red face. Eyes without brows.

"Did I scare you?" she heard him saying. "I'm used to it. Since the civilized Germans turned me into a scarecrow, I lie in wait like a wolf among sheep. But don't be afraid, a Jewish wolf doesn't bite." He laughed. Janet forced herself to smile.

"Do you like goulash?" he asked.

"Goulash in a French restaurant?"

"We're not going to a French restaurant. We're going to a Hungarian restaurant — my restaurant. The best restaurant in New York."

"Why not a French restaurant?" Janet asked with forced cheer.

"Because I can't stand how the hoity-toity French wipe their plates with their bread."

The Hungarian restaurant was warm, bright, pleasant. The glare of an unseen sun was reflected in freshly washed windows. Where did the rain go? she wondered. She struggled not to look at the black toupee sliding down his forehead — or maybe she just imagined she wasn't looking.

"Don't be concerned," he said of his appearance. "Worse things happened, and the world was silent." He spoke of his horrific experiences in a relaxed tone, as if he were talking not about himself but about someone with whom he had no connection.

Janet felt she had to say something, a word, an expression of sympathy. She was still in shock. Of all the possibilities, she hadn't expected an encounter like this one. She sat and looked over his head to the spring evening outside, searching there for the words that could free her tongue for relaxed conversation.

The poet called the waiter and ordered goulash. She asked for a black coffee.

"That's all?" he asked as if she had insulted him.

"Maybe later," Janet says. "First, coffee." Now she saw sunglasses perched on his nose. They covered his naked eyelids and made it easier to look at him. She even attempted a smile.

The poet leaned over the table. "By the way, what's your name?"

"Janet. Janet Silver."

"Tell me, Janet, would you mind if I called you Gitele?"

"Why Gitele?"

"Gitele means more to me. Just this morning I wrote a poem dedicated to my sister Gitele. I believe it's quite a good one."

"You're a prolific writer then?"

"Do I have a choice? When the heart dictates and the pen is willing, one writes. Do you know what I mean, Gitele?"

"No, I don't."

"I know women who when asked a yes-or-no question respond with an entire paragraph. From you, my dear, it's hard to extract a simple yes or no."

"It may seem that way," Janet said, "but I'm just waiting for the coffee to take effect. Meanwhile I'd very much like to hear your poem."

"I don't remember it by heart."

"Do you remember the title?"

"The title is not important."

"What is, then?"

"It depends. For some poets, it's the syntax, the music, the rhyme. For me it's the main idea, how it emerges from the depths of the imagination, naked, raw, without form, without shape, but with a yearning to become the visual expression of one's innermost drive."

Janet sipped and considered the poet. She'd never tasted such extraordinary coffee. Across from her, the poet was eating his goulash. Fat oozed over his lips. But his terrible appearance and sloppy table manners no longer bothered her. She wanted to know the person underneath the skin. She wanted to feel what he felt, what he suffered, what he thought. For his part, he was trying to penetrate her thoughts.

But all he could see was the external: her face worn, her body full-figured and promising.

"You still haven't told me the theme of this morning's poem."

The poet shoved his plate aside. He wiped his lips and pushed his dark glasses up, then immediately pulled them back down. "My theme," he said, "is Moses, Moses our teacher."

"With or without horns?" she asked calmly.

"My Moses is not an exhibitionist. He wears his horns on the inside. He struggles with man and with God. My Moses insists on speaking to God face to face. He has much to ask, much to say. When God says that a human being cannot see His face and remain alive, Moses still insists. He accepts the possibility of a horrible death for a single glimpse of his Creator."

The poet mopped the sweat from his brow. He removed his hat and laid it on the chair beside him. His face was as red as embers; his lips glistened. He opened his napkin and brushed a fleck from his lapel. His eyes behind the black glasses gleamed with poetic self-confidence. He took her hand across the table and brought it to his lips. "Don't you think the weather has cleared up beautifully?" he said. A broad but ambiguous smile appeared on his face.

"Is that what you're thinking about?"

"No," he responded. "Civilized people do not discuss what they're thinking."

"What's holding you back? I'm an adult and quite used to hot and cold."

"You're sure?"

"A hundred percent sure."

"The truth is that I'd like to invite you up to my place on the third floor. I live here. This is my building, my restaurant."

"You're joking."

"No, I'm not joking. A person has to make a living. You can't make a living from poetry. I want to introduce you to my creativity, my true self, what makes me tick."

"Not today," Janet responded. "I have a headache."

A heavy silence fell over the table, enshrouding them in a private fog. Around them guests were talking and laughing. A red sunset colored the windowpanes. After a long moment, the poet leaned over the table and in a steamy voice said directly into her face: "Excuse me for disappointing you. No doubt you were expecting a Byron, a poet in a black cape with a red lining. You hoped he would overwhelm you, take you by force. Perhaps you wanted him to kidnap you, to rape you. You'd ride his chariot into the pages of books, into the realm of literary celebrity. Pardon me, Janet, if I'm mistaken. The truth is that we both deluded ourselves. I waited for you with great excitement. I had a vague premonition I would re-experience the same shiver that made me a poet long ago. I hoped that as we grew closer we would discover things that were unknown perhaps even to ourselves. But you arrived all upset and scattered, without the little red umbrella. Maybe that's why we're so out of sorts, without knowing why."

Janet's fixed her gaze on her wet shoes. A heavy sadness overtook her. She felt as if she were sealed inside a bell jar. A feeling of humility compelled her to close her eyes, to spirit herself away to some dark house of prayer. There she pleaded without words, without tears, like a worm wriggling after being cut in two. She wanted to plead for herself, for him, for the shattered human soul, for the contradictory feelings that thrust her forward and then held her back. She knew that his appearance ought not to drive her away. She also knew that the only reason she could consider keeping company with such a burned skull and singed eyes was that she too was born a Jew.

Janet picked up the broken umbrella and laid it in her lap. There was nothing more to say. It was no longer important to change his opinion of her. With sealed lips she understood him better. With closed eyes she saw him more clearly. He was the eternal Jew whom even death could not annihilate. When his face was burned, his soul ascended. A caricature on the outside, a poet within. He'd survived all the calumny, all the pogroms. History had rendered him immortal.

Her Last Dance

When Simone Bonmarchais, the police chief's mistress, entered the elegant cabaret on the Champs-Élysées that evening, the regulars immediately noted the change that had come over her. A strange and unfamiliar expression had spread over her face like a shadow, wiping away both her smile and her pride and leaving only the cool composure that came with her position.

Women whispered to one other at the crowded tables, glancing at their companions with probing eyes in an attempt to convey without words the impression that the blond mademoiselle had made on them. No one dared to speak out loud. It was no secret that the place was swarming with undercover agents, and no one wanted to tangle with the police chief.

That evening the police chief and his blond lover were accompanied by the Gestapo agent Herr Gruber and his assistant, Fritz Untermeier. In fact, it was the Gestapo agent himself who had invited the couple. The blond mademoiselle had tried hard to decline the invitation, but without success. She couldn't bear the Gestapo agent, but not because of his job — she was already quite accustomed to entertaining the German invaders. No, Herr Gruber was repugnant for more personal reasons. First, he never had a complimentary word for her. Whenever he spoke to her, he looked over her head, as if intentionally avoiding eye contact. His antipathy toward her made him even uglier in her eyes than he actually was. People said he harbored an intense hatred of French women. For his sexual needs he used young German women, although even with them he never exchanged words. A woman, for him, was less than human, nothing more than the wench of medieval times. He said very little, but when he did speak, he compelled the listener, with his myopic eyes, to look directly at him. Even in the company of friends, he was stiff, cold, and aloof. The brass buttons on his fitted uniform glittered with a sinister superiority. The scar on his face spoke of his heroism and also reflected his moods. At the slightest agitation, it flared up like a bloody saber on his right side and spread from his ear to the corner of his mouth.

In contrast to Herr Gruber, his assistant Untermeier devoured women with his eyes, his hands, and even his feet. He submitted utterly to the will of his Gestapo boss, fulfilling his commands like clockwork. But when it came to women, he was an independent actor. Even here at the table, while he was engrossed in translating a German report into French, his foot was toying with that of the beautiful mademoiselle sitting across from him.

Mlle. Bonmarchais was absorbed in herself. Looking in the mirror, she was fascinated by her own image. She was in love with her appearance; it was the passport that allowed her to cross borders that were sealed off to others. Now she attended to her face, patting a curl into place, applying lipstick and eye shadow. She plied the pencil with nimble fingers: the darker the coloring, the more brightly her eyes shone with the sparks of erotic embers. She could feel the sparks in her finger tips, tingling down her back all the way to her feet, with which the assistant Untermeier was seeking to connect. She stood up, then sat back down. The flame she was fanning inside herself was not for him, but for a notion she was about to act upon.

The conversation at the table was in German, which Mlle. Bonmarchais did not understand. She caught a few words she remembered from her Yiddish-speaking parents. M. Durand, the police chief, did not know, nor did he suspect in his wildest dreams, that his lover was Jewish. He was speaking in a low voice. His face was as taut and sallow as parchment. The nervous tics around the right corner of his mouth testified to the seriousness of the discussion.

Among the full and empty glasses on the table were scattered newspapers in various languages. It was the summer of 1944. The Allies had landed on the golden beaches of Normandy. This new situation placed the bleached blond mademoiselle in a dilemma. The worm of doubt that lurked within every turning point had crawled into her pampered soul. Simone did not believe in principles; she led her life by caprice alone. In fact, one could say that principles played no part in her life at all. She relied on her intuition to take her from one stage to the next, even into the bedroom. Now her intuition was whispering that it was time to turn over a new leaf.

Her dreams, too, had changed drastically. The erotic had given way to the nightmare. Night after night, she dreamed about a path without an exit. She wandered in a garden with tortuous footpaths, bounded by trimmed bushes like the ones in the garden at Versailles. She knew the way, having been there before in so many dreams. To arrive at her destination, she had to cross the bridge. But the way was complicated; the footpaths snaked out in all directions, leading to the nooks where courtesans used to receive the men of the royal entourage. She left traces so that she wouldn't lose her way, but the gardener with his long broom swept them away. She stumbled into a strange neighborhood. The streets were narrow, dark, dead. She turned as if in a labyrinth. The gutters on both sides of the street overflowed with windblown newspapers and glass from smashed windowpanes. All the doors were nailed shut with boards defaced by swastikas. She realized she must be in Belleville. Somewhere on rue Ramponeau was the Jewish bakery where her mother used to buy apple strudel and sponge cake. Now the bakery was boarded up and covered with brown swastikas. A German soldier with a rifle on his shoulder strolled back and forth. Under a lamppost swayed a small sign with the inscription: "Belleville: Free of Jews."

Simone remembered the dream. It came to her in various incarnations, and she responded by embracing luxury and danger.

This very morning she had carried out a daring mission. She had smuggled out an R.A.F. flier who had escaped from custody and delivered him to the Resistance. She had hidden the flier in her maid's attic quarters, dressed his wounds, provided him with civilian clothes and a false passport, and driven him in her car to his destination. Simone Bonmarchais worked only for prominent men, wanting nothing to do with ordinary people. She was the ideal mistress for her lover, as she asked no favors of him. Underlings did the preparatory work, providing her with the passports and warning her of danger. She rewarded them with higher positions and better pay. With an aesthetic outlook, she dismissed the rumors of mass murder. In her bleached blond head, such outrageous stories could not take up residence. The scope of the atrocity was so far beyond human comprehension that lies were more believable than truth.

Simone was well aware of the retaliatory actions carried out by the occupying forces, however. For each German killed, dozens of French people were lined up against the wall and shot. "That's the nature of war!" M. Durand tried to explain to his associates. "When the shooting stops, everything will return to the way it was."

In the Élysée nightclub the light projector turned, swirling the colors of the rainbow over the heads of the guests. The music of the dance hall grated on everyone's nerves. Mlle. Bonmarchais's full bosom rose and fell to the beat of the music. Her white throat dazzled the eye. A single rose, its petals still closed, adorned her towering coiffure. In her mind, she contrasted her lover, the French police chief, opaque and resigned, with the English officer, so full of courage and hope. Looking at M. Durand, she felt herself to be an outsider. Truth be told, she had always felt like an outsider in his eyes. She had looked into his heart as if through a crack. Now that crack was closing. She didn't know if he planned to flee with the enemy or stay behind in France and live incognito. Either way, what had been was no more. That chapter in her life had come to an end.

Simone's parents had emigrated from Warsaw. She herself had been born in Paris. As a child she used to dress up in the fantastic rags that filled the house — the used clothes, shoes, hats, and silk underwear that her father purchased from the wealthy homes along the grand boulevards. He walked the streets with a sack on his shoulders, singing out in French: "*Marchand d'habits, chiffons!*" Windows would open and women would thrust out their tousled heads. Some tossed down their rags for free. Others invited him up and turned over a sealed bundle in exchange for money. Her mother sorted everything out, sewing on buttons, mending holes, and removing stains. On weekends she would lay out her wares at the *marché*. She attracted customers with the melody of Warsaw in her voice. Her accent did her business no harm; at the Marché Saint-Antoine, all the accents swirled together: Algerian, Polish, Chinese, Russian. Even gullible Americans came looking for bargains.

Little Simone was raised by a French nanny. She absorbed the nanny's customs and the sing-song cadences of her speech. The nanny imbued in her a love for the golden age when great kings in powdered wigs ruled the land. For hours on end, the little girl listened to stories of the ladies-in-waiting who controlled politics from behind the scenes. She knew almost nothing of Jewish history, and later, when she could have read about it on her own, it was of little interest to her. Marie Antoinette's bitter demise moved her more deeply than the pogroms in Czarist Russia.

She was seventeen years old when she was hired as a secretary to a certain M. Legrand, one of the biggest fruit wholesalers at Les Halles, the central market in Paris. For him, a young woman was like fresh fruit just fallen from the tree. It didn't take long for M. Legrand to make the young Simone an offer, and she didn't allow the chance to slip away. From the novels she had read and the stories told by her nanny, she knew that opportunity did not come knocking twice. For their first rendezvous they selected a discreet hotel deep in the Bois de Boulogne. She waited for him in a private room furnished in the style of Louis XIV with Persian carpets underfoot, heavy curtains on the windows, bouquets of flowers, and paintings on the wall. Music played softly. Porters in red uniforms and white gloves popped the champagne cork with great ceremony. Simone's behavior was so convincing that no one could have guessed that this was her first tryst. Even the sophisticated M. Legrand was amazed at how willingly she gave away her virginity, as if it were a longstanding burden.

M. Legrand fell genuinely in love with her. He made no secret of his married life with his wife and children. Simone accepted it all as par for the course. During the three years of their affair she matured into a true coquette. She lived at his expense in her own apartment. She changed her name from Bratlovski to Bonmarchais, took private lessons from a professor at the Sorbonne, and shopped for clothes on Saint-Honoré. Expensive cosmetics and visits to beauty salons became an essential habit.

Her parents kept their daughter's behavior a secret. Each blamed the other. If she had been sent to Jewish schools and met other Jewish young people, such a calamity might never have befallen her. Now her parents had no more influence over her. They hoped that when her true match appeared on the scene, he and the engagement ring would cover up her current actions.

At the same time that Simone carried on with M. Legrand, she was also having an affair with a diplomat from the American embassy, who kept her up-to-date on the political intrigues. He introduced her to the titans of the age, the ones who amused themselves by deciding the fate of the world.

Simone did not give up her friendship with M. Legrand, however. From time to time they still met in the hotel where the peacocks on the wall, with their brightly colored fans, kept the fires of their first night burning. Nor did it bother her that the diplomat offered her no engagement ring. The world stood on the brink of a catastrophe. The uncertainty of tomorrow made today more intense; seizing the pleasure of the moment was the order of the day.

Paris fell. The mighty Maginot Line gave up the ghost without a whimper. French pride, fatally wounded, lay in a stupor. The conqueror sought and found collaborators willing to serve the *Herrnfolk*. M. Durand, who had sided with the political right wing throughout his political career, found favor in their eyes and was promoted to the position of chief of police.

By this point, the newly appointed police chief had already taken Simone Bonmarchais as his lover. He saw her as the embodiment of the eternal feminine essence. Here was a woman who drew her spiritual sustenance from fashion magazines. Her favorite heroes were the ladies in the royal boudoirs of yesteryear. More than once he reflected that she had been born into the wrong time.

Simone Bonmarchais was content with his opinion of her. It gave her the opportunity to look and see without being seen. Indeed, in the smoke-filled, champagne-soaked nightclub, she looked and saw that the end was nigh. Tonight she was preparing to put an end to the liaison that was no longer sustainable. The feelings that she had once had for her lover had long since died out. All that remained was emptiness. And since her temperament could not bear emptiness of any kind, she planned to make a dramatic farewell right here at the table. She would pretend to be drunk, she decided, and would show her cards with a glass of bubbly in hand. She would even hint at her Jewish origins. It would be interesting to see how her lover would react. And what would Herr Gruber, the Gestapo agent, say? She would allow her words to drift this way and that. One moment she would be a Jewish woman; the next, the great-great-grandchild of Mme. Pompadour. In her imagination she could see herself scaling dizzying heights. Her face burned with the drama of the moment.

Herr Gruber observed her from behind his dark glasses. He didn't approve of the way she lit one cigarette after another, slurped her wine, and painted her face. He had long suspected that the overly pretty mademoiselle was playing a double role. He was sorry not to have taken steps to deal with the matter earlier. Now he could no longer delay: she had to be eliminated, soon, perhaps even tonight.

"Why don't you invite the mademoiselle to dance?" He turned suddenly to his adjutant. "They say you're an expert when it comes to fancy footwork."

Fritz Untermeier was quite pleased with the unexpected invitation. He quickly laid his papers in his briefcase and gathered up the scattered newspapers, meanwhile forgetting that one of his shoes was under the table. The mademoiselle burst into loud laughter. She was still laughing when her gaze snagged on a familiar name. "Marcel Legrand" jumped out from a small notice in *Paris Soir*. Her former lover, her first. She brought the newspaper to her eyes, but couldn't make out anything. Rings of fire encircled the table, the hall. His name fluttered around the fire, unhurt, like moths on a summer night. "M. Marcel Legrand," she read over and over, "a wholesale merchant at Les Halles, was shot tonight for delivering poisoned food to the German army."

Mlle. Bonmarchais flapped her hands like a shot bird. "*Sale boche!*" she spat. The Germans didn't hear the oath directed against them, or perhaps pretended not to. M. Durand, the police chief, shuffled the newspaper toward himself. He knitted his heavy brows and appraised his lover with a dark look. "Who is this man — an acquaintance of yours? A friend?"

"An acquaintance and a friend!" she answered, now entirely calm. Surprised by her boldness, she felt a profound contentment, as if she had just been freed from some abstract burden. It didn't bother her that her answer had exploded like a bomb in the room. Let it lead where it would. Every victory had its casualties. Her victory had brought her back to herself.

M. Durand drained his glass. "How is it that I've never heard his name?"

"Maybe I didn't consider him important enough to mention!" Simone replied. Her white hands fluttered around her face, busy with the rose in her hair. She flashed a coquettish smile at Herr Gruber, who did not return it or respond. His eyes behind the black glasses were unblinking. Only the scar on his face blazed with all the fires of hell. He stood, tightened his belt, fingered his medals. "We'll be right back," he said, and was off to the telephone booth with his assistant.

When he returned, his face exuded pride, giving no indication that he had just signed a death sentence. He even brought two fire-red carnations for the mademoiselle. He tried making a joke, but no one laughed. "Just so," he said in an entirely different tone. "We have more significant matters to attend to than lovers' heartaches. If the fraulein is not opposed, Untermeier will see to it that she is not bored."

Once the Gestapo agent was left alone with his French collaborator, he drew closer to him. "Don't despair, Herr Inspector," he said. "You haven't heard the last word yet. German minds work methodically. An atomic bomb will soon offer us the world on a platter."

M. Durand tried to hold his gaze. "It's not so easy to lie in the wolf's mouth and wait for secret weapons," he said.

"You won't have to wait much longer, Herr Durand. We Germans don't postpone for tomorrow what we can do today." The Gestapo agent removed his glasses and regarded his collaborator through narrowed eyes. "How long have you known your girlfriend — Fraulein Bonmarchais, that is?" His tone filled the Frenchman with unease. M. Durand bit his lips. His face turned pale. "Herr Gruber," he said, "if you suspect my bride, you suspect me as well. It's possible she did know the dealer from Les Halles who was eliminated. But that doesn't mean she herself is involved in the treachery. I too know people on the other side. All of Paris did not change overnight. You must understand that my bride is completely apolitical. In short, we intend to be married."

"Well then, I wish you all the best!" said Herr Gruber. He put his glasses back on and proposed a toast. A waiter came and filled their glasses. "We'll build the thousand-year reign together yet. Take my word for it, Herr Inspector." He lifted his glass. "To friendship! To victory!"

They sat for a moment in silence. "Don't despair, Durand, my friend," the Gestapo agent said. "All will be well again. I know what I'm talking about. The new weapon will accomplish in just a few days the victory that three years of war couldn't achieve!"

"For whose benefit?" the Frenchman asked.

"For our benefit, of course."

Simone Bonmarchais allowed herself to be led to the dance floor.

She needed time to sift through her thoughts. Her plans were in a muddle. What she had been thinking an hour ago was no longer relevant. The role of the drunk that she had been playing now seemed laughable. At this point, her thoughts were focused exclusively on Marcel Legrand. What had he been thinking at the moment of death? Maybe he hadn't been thinking about death at all. Perhaps he felt that giving his life for the homeland was a privilege. She wanted, no, she had to see him. She would ask Fritz Untermeier to take her to the La Santé prison. She wanted to breathe the air that had absorbed his last scream. She wanted to stand and look at his corpse that was displayed naked to terrify the citizenry. She herself was unafraid. She felt within herself the strength to overcome death itself.

As she danced, she pressed her bosom against Untermeier's rigid chest. His body trembled. The dance went on and on. Fluttering her eyelids, she confided her request. Fritz Untermeier promised to do all that she asked, although he knew that he would not do what she wanted, but what the chief commanded. Now he was waiting for final authorization. When the waiter handed him a sealed envelope, he abruptly stopped dancing. His face changed color. "Come!" he said. "We must leave the hall."

Simone Bonmarchais gave him a flirtatious look. "What's happened? Has your victorious army surrendered?"

Again his face changed color, from red to white and back to red. "We Germans do not surrender!" he said in a hard tone she hadn't heard before. "Get your purse, Mademoiselle, and come with me. There is no time for discussion."

"Is that an order?"

"Call it what you will. We must go. At once."

"I need to know where we're going, or else I'm staying here."

"You're coming with me. I am responsible for your safety."

"Who appointed you my guardian?"

"The one with whom you make love."

"I don't believe it."

"Believe it or not. That is your privilege. But you must come at once."

"Show me the order. I need to see who signed it!"

"The order was given to me, not to you."

"I'm not going!"

"Then I'll take you out by force."

"I'll make a scene!"

"Go ahead. No one will come to your aid."

"I don't need help. I can stand on my two feet."

"I've no doubt about that. Come along, Mademoiselle," he said in a softer voice. "It's a splendid night; anything is possible."

"I have a revolver, Monsieur Fritz."

"I don't duel with women."

"Then may I go to the ladies' room?"

"If you must, but only if I go with you."

"You're joking."

"Not at all. You fail to grasp the seriousness of the situation."

"What situation? The front? Or is this a personal vendetta?"

"My dear fraulein, you're too charming to argue with. But an order is an order." He took her by the arm and led her outside. Two S.S. men were waiting. They settled the fraulein into the car and drove from the Champs-Élysées to the Place de Concorde, passing the elegant restaurants where she and M. Legrand had once been so happy. From there the car turned deeper into the woods, where a single bullet dyed her blond hair a hideous shade of red.

Waiting for the Ragman

After all these years, I'm still lugging the past behind me — the house, the street, the village, the town. Enough! I tell myself. What's done is done. Turn over a new leaf, look at the sprouts coming up in the garden. "The rain is over and gone. . . . The voice of the turtle is heard in our land." I prick up my ears and hear not the turtledove but the descending notes of the nightingale, a kaleidoscope of song. Overtone struggles with undertone, rhythm tangles with rhythm, sound overtakes sound — a fugue without a conductor.

I sit in my fortress by the half-open window. Early spring reigns over the world. Songs from across the border flutter in the breeze, soaring over the river, up the mountain, and in through the half-open window, straight to me. How could I have turned away from a song that was sung for neither money nor applause but simply for the rosy spring evening that lingered late into the mysterious night?

It was the gentiles in the village who sang this song — the same villagers who carried shiny knives in their bootlegs when they went to church on Sunday. Early on, the keenness of their knives and the magic of their songs nestled together in my soul, the two elements side by side like a self divided.

There were those who viewed the paradox of knife and song as an inheritance passed down directly from primeval man to his modern descendants. Among those holding this opinion was Yosip, the enlightened son of peasants who returned from the big city with three silver stripes on his stiff collar. He couldn't share the elevated ideas he'd acquired at school with the gentile girls in the village, but one day he crossed the bridge and climbed the hill to the Jewish street. There he came upon the youngest daughter of the synagogue sexton, a dark-haired beauty of sixteen whose plump cheeks were adorned with charming dimples. Her appearance was deceiving. While other girls engaged in love affairs, she sustained herself with fat volumes of fiction. That fine morning, Sorke noticed a shadow falling over her open book. She looked up to find Yosip standing with one foot on the stoop where she was sitting. Glancing back at her book, she imagined that the figure towering over her was none other than Raskolnikov, the hero of *Crime and Punishment*, with a knife under his jacket. She stood up quickly, prepared to run away, but he blocked her path.

"Pardon me, young lady," " he said, not in Raskolnikov's hesitant tones but with a raw, hard Ukrainian accent, "is that Dostoyevsky I see you reading?"

"I'm not reading," she demurred, "just looking."

The excitement of their first meeting lasted through two whole summers. Sorke clutched to her heart the flowers he brought from his father's garden. He presented her with golden ears of corn, too, and blood-red strawberries. Between kisses, he told her he was reading *The Nazarene*, by the controversial Sholem Asch. Heart aflutter, she fixed on him the dazzling black eyes that filled half her face and every inch of her soul.

Before returning to the big city to continue his instruction in the ways of the world, Yosip presented her with a watch with black hands. She fastened the leather band around her wrist. Every time she set the watch ahead, the hands turned backward of their own accord. When they reached midnight, Sorke was standing before an open pit. Naked, ashamed, more dead than alive, she was waiting for someone, she knew not whom. A direct descendant of primeval man ripped the watch off her wrist. Dressed in a brown uniform and white gloves, he whistled a melody that had once moved her to tears.

I don't know whether the melody reached her consciousness, or whether she continued to hope that he would appear before her, reach a hand across the border, and assure her that humanity was not coming to an end.

If he had gone to his death with her, I would have sung a song of praise and the load on my shoulders would have sprouted wings. If God's wrath had poured down upon everyone equally, devouring all without exception, bird and beast and fish in the sea and all the plants on the face of the earth, had a flood swallowed up one and all regardless of race or religion, then the poison in my heart would have turned to manna. I would have regarded the Holocaust with reverence. I would have bowed down to nature and her whims, lowering myself into the mouth of the abyss and grasping the whys and wherefores without needing to ask. But what man has done to man — this I cannot forgive. How am I to say Kaddish for a town, a people, for young and old, strong and weak, for the beautiful and the ugly, the devout and the thieves? How to say the blessing for the souls of crazy Hershele and blind Khatzkele, perhaps the only ones who stood by that open grave without knowing pain or shame?

Sometimes I think I might be crazy, deluded, melancholic. To keep the madhouse at bay, I dig into my load of memories and begin to cast off the yesterdays that weigh so heavily on the present. I'm not particular — I throw out whatever I can get my hands on. But the more I discard, the more accumulates. I reach down to the very bottom, and up comes a band of beggars. I had no idea they were still alive somewhere in my consciousness, each with his particular disease or deformity. Every Monday they would show up at the market and take their places near the town hall, one with amputated feet, another with a scrofulous face, each beseeching the passersby for alms in his own way. One strummed a lyre and sang a sad song. Another carried a monkey on his shoulder that pulled a fortune ticket out of a box when handed a coin. The one I was drawn to was the blind gentile woman. I liked to listen to her talk about heaven, where angels with white wings were watching over her, preparing a table for her in the world above, where her true life would begin. She was certain that Jesus himself would restore her sight. She would look down from on high and pray for the sinners below.

Summer and winter alike, she could be found in her accustomed spot under Aunt Rokhl's window. She sat on a low stool with her petticoat touching the ground, a brass cross dangling on her bosom and a string of beads in her hand. She didn't thank people for the alms they offered. Even when an urchin swiped the *groshns* from her box, words continued to stream from her mouth like lava from a volcano. Her lips were dry, her eyes like two empty saucers, her voice as keen as the sword of the Angel of Death who reigns over the devils in hell.

It was said that her own father had put out her eyes when she was a child. In the years of famine, parents did cripple their children, their wives, even themselves, chopping off an ear, a foot, or a hand in order to stay alive by arousing the sympathy of those with a crust of bread to spare.

The blind woman's dance of death had a profound effect on me. Precisely at midday, when the sun reached its highest point and the clock atop the town hall struck twelve, she would rise from her stool, grope for an empty spot, and begin to dance. The laughter and groans that her wild performance called forth from the crowd did not perturb her. Her petticoat dragged in the mud and the cross bounced at her heart as she performed her clumsy routine. She danced until she tumbled face first onto the ground. Her hands and feet twitched spasmodically, her teeth clenched, and a white lather frothed at her mouth. Then she would stand up, find her stool, and pick up where she'd left off with her beads.

Now, years later, in moments of fear, I, too, find myself standing up and dancing — not necessarily at noon or at midnight, but whenever time stops and begins to run backward, like the black hands on Sorke's watch. I dance until I swoon. Then I get back up and go on toward whatever fate may bring my way.

There were Jewish beggars, too. Rather than going to the market, they went from house to house. The men came on Fridays, the women on Saturday mornings. Since no money was allowed to change hands on the Sabbath, they carried baskets and accepted charity in the form of bread and challah. There were some who hid their poverty. Instead of going from house to house themselves, they dispatched the wives of the synagogue sextons to fill their baskets for them. The higher the pedigree of these women, the more generously people would give. The most highborn would receive a whole loaf or an egg. A household with a cow could contribute a bottle of milk, a pat of butter, or perhaps a spoonful of jam.

The poor introduced a certain element of diversion into the house, not so much for the adults as for the girl who was, the girl whose tides ebb and flow on my sandy shores to this day. I sit at her side by the frosted window, looking through her eyes as black ravens dance on white snow. Staring deep into the whiteness makes me sad, and so I linger there for a bit, content to be sitting beside her. She takes me under her wing and we become one.

There is much to think about, much to feel, on these short winter days that have no end. I have an idea. Suppose she and I were to change the order of the days of the week. Between Hanukkah and Passover, the week would start not with Sunday or Monday but with Thursday, the day when preparations for the all-important Sabbath begin.

Thursday is when Mother goes shopping. With her oilcloth bag, she goes from one store to the next, buying something from each of Father's customers in turn. Left alone at home, the girl rummages through the drawers she's not allowed to open. She knows where Mother keeps her girlhood brassieres, her silk garters, the bar of aromatic soap and the empty perfume bottle. She leafs through old fashion magazines, looking at the models with their exotic hairstyles. She sniffs the soap and tries on the brassieres full of forbidden secrets.

When darkness falls, she shuts the drawers and takes her place at the window to wait for Mother. Often the windows are so thick with frost that not even a shadow seeps through. She huddles by the oven, even though it's as cold as she is, and begins counting to a hundred. As she starts off with the number one, she can see Mother, just as I do now, coming out of red-headed Khane's shop. She walks slowly, picking her way through the wet snow, her oilcloth bag overflowing with good things. We don't stop to list these things but continue counting, she and I, until we come to the number fifty, by which time Mother has reached the Great Synagogue. There the sidewalk is dry and her pace quickens. We see her lifting her dress just so as she descends the steps and makes her way to the lower street. Now she is passing the Black Tailor's hut. Here we hope against hope that she won't encounter the tailor's wife, in which case all our counting will have been in vain. When we reach a hundred and she's still not at home, we start over. Maybe in our haste we skipped a number. We have no choice but to begin again.

The minute she walks in, all's right with the world. The house grows warm and bright as heavenly aromas rise from her bag. We're allowed a taste of everything she unpacks: a prune, a lick of sugar, a raisin, a drop of honey. We sniff the yeast, the cinnamon, the saffron, even the pepper. After so many rich experiences, we're fast asleep before Father arrives home from the butcher shop.

They come to me still in my dreams, those exalted days and nights. I see the girl set in an idyll embroidered with light blue thread. Having no dolls, she draws one with her finger on a cloudy pane. In summer she chases after butterflies and sings with the wind. Because she's an only daughter, Mother keeps her inside all winter. Alone within the four walls, she creates her own world with its own orderly rules and a special function for each day. Friday is full, with so many things to do: the candlesticks must be polished along with the mortar and pestle and the Hanukkah lamp. Mother opens the door for the poor people and makes sure there is milk for all. A crusty flatbread is baking in the oven. Next will come the knishes, the cookies, and the honey cake.

After the blessing of the candles, Father brings in his Sabbath guest. Some guests eat silently, no doubt thinking of their humble Sabbath tables back home, far off in the countryside. Others recount terrible tales of pogroms from which they escaped by the grace of God. They tell stories of rabbis, of miracles and wonders. Engraved in my memory is a story about a young woman who died in child-birth. The dead body was placed in a tub of hot water and com-manded to deliver up the little soul within. Ten men, including the guest who was telling the story, recited psalms. Women wailed. The midwife paced back and forth in front of the dead body. "Give up the child," she commanded, "and you will be buried as a God-fear-ing Jewish woman deserves."

The image of the dead woman in the bathtub stays with me even in sleep. Only the aromas of the Holy Sabbath soothe me early the next morning when Marina comes in to light the stove. She brings with her the smell of her brown bread, the whiskey on her breath, and the manure on her boots. Later, the poor women arrive. In place of money they take the bread and challah and gulp down a cup of hot coffee in the doorway. We wait for our own special poor person, a young girl whose parents have died and left her to care for all the orphan children. Mother says they live without heat or light. Besides challah, we add to her basket a piece of meat, a little carrot pudding, and some clothes we've outgrown. The girl takes everything, saying only "Good Sabbath."

After the stew and the pudding, the house grows quiet. Father lies down in his clothes on the bench by the stove. All the wood has burned up; only ashes are smoldering. Mother receives guests. "Enjoy! Enjoy!" she says as she serves tea and cookies. While the women talk, the little one looks at her reflection in the brass candlesticks. On the Sabbath she looks different. Instead of a little girl, she becomes a rich lady, adorned like the ones in the magazines hidden in Mother's drawer. She decks herself out in velvet and silk and drapes a white veil over her brown locks. The candlesticks she's polished so fervently sustain her dream until sunset.

Sunday is a day of idleness that feels like the calm before a storm. In the evening, there's nothing left to do but brush Father's long jacket and hang it up in the closet. Then the storm arrives in the form of the Monday market. The girl and I part. I leave her at home, still spellbound, and slip in through the open door at Aunt Rokhl's. She and my grandmother run a one-day restaurant for the market folk. Each customer receives a bowl of soup containing a quarter of a roast chicken with parsnip, dill, and other delicious things whose fragrance fills the house and wafts out into the market square. The customers are mostly sellers from surrounding towns. When business is going well, along with their soup they order a serving of jellied calf's foot and a glass of whiskey that Aunt Rokhl serves under the table. They sit at a long board on long narrow benches, leaning back against the two made-up beds.

How I remember these robust Jews with their frost-covered beards who guzzled their soup and sucked the bones, not forgetting to pinch Aunt Rokhl's behind as she brought the food to the table.

The restaurant was open only in winter. In summer, when the peasants were busy in the fields and the market slumbered, Aunt Rokhl made her living by sewing wedding gowns. One summer, she got married. The groom was one of her steady customers whose wife had died during the winter. He walked in one day and found my aunt at her machine at work on someone's gown. "Pack your bags," he commanded, giving her ample flesh a squeeze. "It's time you tasted of the Tree of Life." He spent the night with a relative in town, and on Monday evening after the market a wedding canopy was erected. Then the couple packed up and left town. My grandmother packed up, too, and moved in with us.

My grandmother was a little woman of few words. She scurried about the house as quiet as a hen, pecking like a chicken at her meager crusts of bread, which she hid in the pocket of her velvet underskirt. It took her a long time to finish chewing a single mouthful. When the dietary laws allowed, she dipped the bread in warm milk.

She knew how to cook and to bake, but in our house she only washed dishes. She rarely spoke and never told me stories. Only after she died did I learn that she had been abandoned as a child. As a ten-year-old orphan, she'd been married off to my grandfather, then twelve, who had been called up as a soldier in the Czar's army. A peasant found them wandering in a field, settled them into his wagon, and drove them straight to the Monday market, where merciful people called a meeting and argued for a long time over what to do. Finally a rich leather merchant with a large household and a sick wife took the couple in and gave them a small space to themselves. The young man, who was educated, tutored the children, starting with the alphabet and continuing on to the Talmud. The ten-year-old wife helped her mistress with the housework.

When my grandfather was eighteen and my grandmother sixteen, she became pregnant. By then they had their own place and her husband was a full-fledged teacher who numbered the children of distinguished people among his students. As long as he was alive, his wife and two daughters did not go hungry, but as soon as he died, they found themselves in a difficult situation. My mother, the elder one, soon married. My grandmother and Aunt Rokhl had no choice but to turn the schoolroom into a restaurant.

All her life, my grandmother remained a child — naïve, frightened, forever seeking a safe corner where she would attract no notice. She did not intervene in my parents' private quarrels or try to discipline her grandchild. And as quietly and modestly as she lived, so she passed away. We never even knew she was ill. At dawn, Father heard her get out of bed. She washed her hands, recited the prayer, went back to bed, and died.

Upon her death, I inherited her velvet underskirt, a couple of shirts full of holes, her tattered slippers, and some moth-eaten dresses. I took this inheritance and stuffed it into the bag of rags I was saving for the ragman.

All the children on our street looked forward to the ragman's visits. He came once a year, on the day before Passover. Most of his trade was with children. For him they filled sacks with rags and bones, rusted pots and broken pieces of iron. I was a millionaire with bones. With every cut of meat my father brought home, he also brought a sack rattling with bones: brittle bones, dried-out bones, brittle old dried-out bones. By the day before Passover, my bag was bulging. The ragman would lift the heavy bundle without stopping to weigh or measure it. Sighing and knitting his bushy brows, he would toss the pack onto his wagon.

In his eyes, everything had value. He rewarded us children with a little wooden horse, a rubber ball, a doll or a storybook, a pinch on the cheek and best wishes for a happy Passover. As soon as he appeared with his horse and wagon, the street came to life. When he rang his bell, the toil-worn housewives came running with their torn blankets, old galoshes, shoes beyond repair. In return, they received a blue goblet for Passover or a glass with a gold rim. These treasures they wrapped in newspaper and stored in the attic from one Passover to the next.

The young Passover sun liked to play with the colored glasses that stood on the sideboard for the holiday. The sunrays admired their reflection in the green vase, in Elijah the Prophet's crimson chalice, in my little blue cup with its dainty handle. All the colors fused together, transmuted into shimmering stars that spangled the white-washed walls, the clay floor, the table with its seder plate and snowy cloth.

When the sun changed direction, I spread my thin fingers and enticed it into the corner where my bed stood. The rays seeped through my fingers as if through a sieve, becoming the flour and bread that nourished me during later migrations. As I lifted my hands in the air, the beams rained down over my head like a golden raisin wine and began to ferment inside me. Unheard tones resounded from the deep. The sun recorded these unwritten notes and I myself composed the lyrics: promise-words for tomorrow, for later, for next Passover when I would be a child again.

I've never stopped playing that game of light and shadow. Wherever I go, it goes with me. To this day I capture handfuls of sunbeams and use them to illuminate the shadows. I imagine that I'm still a child, as naïve and innocent as my grandmother. Like her, I avoid people. And sensing my eccentricity, others stay away.

I still collect bones — not the ones from my father's butcher shop but those that remain in my memory. I'm still waiting for the ragman to come, to take the heavy pack from my bowed shoulders and toss it into his wagon. I'm waiting for him to pinch my cheek the way he used to do and reward me with a sky-blue cup stamped with tiny white flowers. When the time comes, may the long-awaited prophet emerge and reveal himself, and may he answer my prayer with a loud "Amen."

THE TWIN SISTERS

Every spring the twin sisters meet in Abano, a little Italian resort town nestled at the feet of the Apennine Mountains. The sisters come together from two opposite poles — one from London, the other from Berlin.

The one from London usually arrives first. She brings treats unavailable in Berlin — kosher salami, salted pretzels, and fatty herring — all the way from Whitechapel, and home-baked onion rolls, the kind they used to make back home in Poland.

The sister from Berlin does not care for sweets. She claims that she herself is sweet enough. And it's true. People are drawn to her like bees to honey. By now the honey is a bit stale, to be sure, but she still commands attention. The blue in her eyes and the gold in her hair, which stood her in such good stead during the years of the Hitler plague, still prove useful. Knowing that her London sister will not touch anything with a German label, she brings nothing with her and purchases all her gifts in Italy. The two have long since let go of their

grudges and put aside their resentments. The bond of their twinship
has remained intact.

The get-togethers have been taking place for quite a number of
years. After they've had a good cry or a good laugh and given each
other a once-over with their eyes, hands, heart and soul, each will
casually inquire: "And how's the family?" — to which the invariable
response is a dry "fine, thanks." Soon thereafter the talk turns to news
of the hotel — which guests have returned and which have switched
to another venue. The one who has arrived earlier reveals that last
year's masseuse has gotten married. Her replacement has fingers like
a pair of pliers. The woman who applies the mud is a real character
who can't stop talking. She keeps it up regardless of whether anyone
understands her. She slaps on the mud, delivers a slap to the behind,
and then "*è finita la commedia*," that's all, folks, and she's gone.

While the sister from London awaits the arrival of the sister from
Berlin, she inspects the beds and smooths out the pillow her sister will
be using. She puts the food in the refrigerator and arranges the other
gifts on the bed. On the table by the window she places a few fresh
flowers and a book she's reading, then sits down to wait.

For the London sister, waiting is a special pleasure. She doesn't have
to account to anyone for her time and can sit with her eyes open or
closed. She can think about everything or nothing at all without feeling she's wasting time. She watches as the sun extends its last rays over
the nearby mountain. An evening melancholy steals down from the
mountain to the empty swimming pool. People are already eating
dinner. She loves to sit here and watch the light struggle with the
shadows until it fades into nothingness. An unseen bird pours out a
serenade. Her sister's last letter hinted that she might be coming with
a friend this time, whether a man or a woman she didn't say.

Recently the Berlin sister's letters have become more mysterious
than informative. The London sister feels that with each passing year

the distance between them is widening, the air cooling. At one time their correspondence was quite spontaneous. If one of them had begun sewing a coat, for example, she would elaborate in great detail on its length and width and enclose a bit of fabric so that her sister could see it with her own eyes, feel it with her own hands. If one of them was redecorating, she would cram the envelope with samples of wallpaper and wait for the other to confirm her selection. Nowadays the letters are brief, particularly the ones from Berlin. They say little and conceal a great deal. The chill blowing from the other side saddens the sister from London. She feels that the thread is straining, even if the knot of their twinship cannot be severed by any force in the world.

The room grows dark. A gnawing wistfulness creeps out of the corners, detaching her from the present moment. She has always been the older sister, born a full hour before the sister from Berlin. What happened in the hour between their births that rendered them so fatefully different? The question appears out of nowhere and pounds at her brain. Is it possible that a single hour could have played such a decisive role? Had their father's character taken the upper hand with the second sister, bringing forth a female version of himself in that last hour of struggle?

No, that was absurd. In the final hour, the embryo was already a finished human being. All that the final hour could have done was to prolong the agony of the woman in labor.

No doubt it was the Hitler plague that led the London sister into the swamp in which she has remained stuck. But even years earlier, her younger sister seemed to possess all the attributes needed to pass through the eye of a needle and emerge unscathed. Yet how could anyone survive the fire that raged for four years and remain undamaged?

Even when they were children, she, Taybele, was the follower, while everyone sought out Rosa's friendship. If witches ever existed, Rosa was probably the last of them. She could throw the ball into the opponent's field and still win the game. First children, then teachers — all of them fell under her spell. She, Taybele, struggled over the homework, and Rosa copied it and passed it off as her own to great acclaim. Even in the concentration camp Rosa was the one who found ways to smuggle in the slice of bread that often made the difference between life and death.

In the concentration camp, no one asked how or from where. Any means of staying alive was considered acceptable. Searching for a way out of a predicament became Rosa's second nature. After liberation, when the survivors paired up, mourner with mourner, leaning on one another for protection against the hostile world, Rosa declared that she would be going to Germany.

"Why?" Taybele asked. "Out of all of the countries in the world, why Germany?"

"I have a reason."

"And what is that reason?"

"It's personal."

"Oh?"

"Yes."

Taybele remembers the painful silence that followed this exchange. She had thought for a long time, and then, "How about this," she'd said finally. "You give up the idea of Germany and I'll break off my engagement. I know you don't like my fiancé. We'll both go to Israel. We can work on a kibbutz the way we once dreamed."

"Go ahead," Rosa said. "You can break your engagement and go to Israel, but not with me. I'm going to Germany."

Rosa made no secret of her aversion to Taybele's betrothed. "We may be twin sisters," she said, "but we live on different planets. You've chosen a groom from another century. He lifts his eyes to the heavens and doesn't see the world around him. He's still mourning the destruction of the Temple in Jerusalem. He recites the Al Khet prayer on the Day of Atonement and thinks that's enough. Whose sins does he think he's atoning for — the murderers or the people they murdered?"

"He's atoning for your sins!" Taybele wanted to reply, but she said nothing. She wished she could tell her sister that she wanted to beat her chest like her fiancé, to clear her conscience for devouring so greedily a spoonful of soup smuggled in in a paper bag, for enjoying a rare egg or roast potato — not daring to ask her sister which cook was spilling his seed on her white body. In the camp, transgressions did not exist. Every sin that served to ward off death was fully justified.

Both sisters passed as Poles. "Jadja," as Rosa was known, worked in the kitchen. Usually the Polish prisoners separated themselves from the *zhides* with a bitter hatred. But because of her speech and her appearance, "Jadja" was accepted to their circle without question, while she, "Bronja" was made to feel invisible. Now Taybele is just looking for a peaceful life. She wants to forget what was. She wants to become, if possible, a normal person. Yet in the so-called free world it is "normal" to deny the very existence of life, of belief, of free will, of God Himself.

And so the London sister sits, thinking of one thing and another. Of all the torment, agony, and torture, all the humiliations and dehumanization that her sister endured, she reflects, nothing affected her so much as the time when their father was forced to clean an outhouse with his bare hands. It began as a bad joke during the very first week of the German invasion. Their father was on his way to prayer services when he was stopped by two Brown Shirts with black swastikas on their sleeves. They led him to an open pit where people relieved themselves.

"What is this?" they asked him.

"Human feces," their father replied.

"It's shit, *Jude*, Jewish shit. Say '*Scheisse!*'" they ordered.

Their father repeated the word.

"Now clean it up, you filthy Jew."

"With what, *Herr Kommandant*?"

"You have two hands. Get to work!"

Their father protested, "Such filth must be doused with kerosene and covered with earth."

"I said clean it up!"

Their father did not budge. "Human beings do not do such things, *Herr Kommandant*. Allow me to bring a shovel and perhaps someone to help me with the work."

"I said use your bare hands. Understand, *Jude*? Your bare hands!"

Their father still did not move.

"Do you dare to defy a German officer?"

"I defy no one. All I ask for is human consideration."

"You'll get your consideration, all right." He spoke to his underling, who went into the synagogue and came out with ten Jews. "You see these ten terrified herring-heads? I'm giving you sixty seconds. If you don't do as I ordered, they'll be killed on the spot, and you, big shot, will bury them and cover them with shit."

Their father, by nature a fastidious man, bent to the stench. He dared not take any chances, not out of fear for his own life but for the lives of the ten Jews.

What happened to their father scarred Rosa forever. She was her father's daughter, the apple of his eye, while she, Taybele, clung to their mother. The rupture in Rosa's sixteen-year-old soul never healed. She became someone who never showed her feelings when faced with any kind of adversity — even death. None of the killings, persecutions, and humiliations that followed seemed to affect her so forcefully. Contemplating that long-ago incident, Taybele understands why her sister had to go to Germany. She wanted to fight fire with fire, to cauterize her wound by humiliating others.

Unwelcome news arrives from Berlin: Rosa is living with a young man from the underworld. Together, they're running a business that traffics in stolen goods. She has appeared in court more than once. It is said that the goods in which she trades consist exclusively of stolen Jewish possessions that Germans appropriated for their personal use. She approaches the maids who work in German homes, then forces the owners to give up the stolen articles — the beautifully engraved spice boxes, the Hanukkah menorahs, the candlesticks, the holy books, the crowns for the Torah scrolls. Taybele asks no questions. She is content to receive a word here and there, an occasional piece of news that stumbles across her doorstep like a drunk home from the pub.

Taybele's husband considers Rosa impure and believes that she should not be permitted to enter a Jewish home. He does not want her shadow to darken his doorway, to breathe the air she breathes, to allow her to touch his children. In his opinion she is a witch, and the Torah states clearly: "A witch shall not be permitted to live." Taybele, on the other hand, considers her sister to be among the *lamed-vovniks* of Jewish lore, one of the thirty-six secret righteous men who hold up the world, in this case in female form. Rosa is risking her life to honor their dead father and perhaps also her slaughtered nation. She did it in captivity, and she does it now as a free person. Her father sacrificed his human dignity in order to save ten Jewish lives. He said later that he would have taken upon himself ten times more suffering, untold suffering, before allowing the savage Nazi to carry out his threat.

Even here, enveloped in peaceful quiet at the window, Taybele finds her eyes filling with tears. She remembers her childhood years, bends down to the two little girls running barefoot outside the house. She kisses the ground where they once stepped. She kisses the heavens, the green pine trees, the blue dusk, all of nature in its innocence. She remembers the long winter nights, when blackness reigned outdoors but the house was ablaze with light. A fire burned in the open fireplace. Mother was cooking dumplings; Father was absorbed in a holy book. The two girls busied themselves at the noodle-board. It was Hanukkah, and guests were coming, laden with gifts. The table was set, and the lamp, lit extra bright for the occasion, swallowed up all the shadows. Everyone was eating and laughing. She was eating, too, and as luck would have it she bit into the trick dumpling. Feathers flew before her eyes as her teeth clamped onto a sticky mixture of bran, pepper, and salt. Everyone laughed. She had wept all night, vexed that it had happened to her and not to Rosa. Now she bends lovingly over that scene, trying to enter, if only for a moment, into the pastoral bliss of that nevermore winter night.

She will share this memory with her sister, Taybele thinks. Perhaps they will both have a good laugh. But since Rosa still hasn't arrived, she turns on the television. The newscaster is promising to show something never seen before. A high-ranking official in a local German council has been found cleaning human excrement with his bare hands. It seems he was blackmailed by a Jewish woman by the name of Rosa Karnovski, who knew something about him that he did not want revealed. He says he had no choice but to obey her command. He was under the influence of cocaine, he says, and didn't know what he was doing.

The Karnovski woman, who is the manager of a restaurant known as "The Red Angel," declares that she has nothing public to say. It is, she says, a personal matter.

A LITTLE SONG FOR A JEWISH SOUL

I often go to Temple Beth Shalom, where as a member of Hadassah I help to prepare luncheons. The temple provides free meeting space to members of community organizations. On the lower level is a kitchen stocked with everything necessary for serving refreshments and brewing coffee.

One day I was setting the tables when three young people appeared in the doorway. They looked around as if they weren't sure they had come to the right place.

"Can I help you with something?" I asked.

"I hope so," one of them said.

All three were wearing leather jackets and tight bleached jeans. They had long hair — two brown, one blond. The blond one was carrying an expensive leather bag.

The bag made me nervous. Who knew what might be inside?

The oldest one stepped forward. "He has a yahrzeit today," he said.

175

He pointed at the blond man, who reddened and looked at his shoes.

"I see," I said. "So what can I do for you?"

"We'd like to talk to the rabbi," the young man said. "His wife was Jewish, you know?"

I regarded the blond man, who looked not yet twenty years old.

"When did your wife pass away?" I asked.

His friend answered for him. "A year ago today."

I showed them the way to the rabbi's office, where they remained for a long time. When they came out, the rabbi escorted them to the door and invited them to come back at six in the evening, when he would arrange for someone to say Kaddish and light a candle for the departed soul.

At six o'clock I returned to the temple. I figured something unusual was going to happen, even by today's standards.

The three young people were seated in the first row, facing the bimah where the Torah was read. They had prayer books open in their laps. They stood up when the congregation stood up and sat down when the congregation sat down.

Whether they were actually looking in the prayer books, I couldn't tell. All I could see was their backs and the yarmulkes perched on top of their long hair. They kept their eyes facing forward. No doubt they could feel the curious eyes trained on them from all sides, but they didn't look around. They didn't move a muscle, as if trying not to spoil their mystical experience.

After an elder member of the congregation had said Kaddish, the blond young man stood up and started to strum his guitar. His two friends stood quietly for a few measures, and then they began to sing the popular tune about the girl who chose an early death because she couldn't cope with life.

The congregation sat as if stunned, hanging on every note to the very end. The sweetness of the song was as tender as a caressing breeze. The young people's voices were magnificent, thrilling.

The moment the concert was over, they were gone without even a goodbye. On the bench where they'd sat they left behind a free pile of phonograph records, and I picked one up. It turned out that the three of them were the original authors of the song, which had sold millions of copies.

At home, I put the record on the turntable and listened again and again, living and reliving the tragedy of the Jewish girl who had fallen in love with the sweet notes flowing from the hot lips of the blond man — he addicted to chemicals, she addicted to his love. Perhaps what sent her over the edge was abandoning her people for unfamiliar territory. Or perhaps it was the green eyes of jealousy.

Perhaps she was a butterfly in the green meadow, driven by longing into the great unknown.

As night fell, her sad Jewish eyes looked out at me from the dark windowpanes, until I turned and lifted the needle from the black disc. Then, to my surprise, I began to recite the mourner's prayer: *yisgadal ve-yiskadash. . . .*

THE INVENTED BROTHER

The day my older brother left home in search of justice was nothing short of a calamity for me. The birds, with their innate sense of oncoming doom, departed their nests and flew away noisily into the empty void and in the middle of the night, the cattle grew restless in their stalls, bellowing and butting the stone walls with their horns.

The shock did not actually come the day he left; it came during the night when — to my own surprise — I found myself beginning to understand the words that he had drummed into me time and time again.

Man is both saint and sinner, my older brother claimed. Today he murders, tomorrow he repents. He does both with great enthusiasm, one could even say with wild enjoyment. It's a kind of masochism for him. He knows he's an abandoned child, a bastard on Mother Earth, so he searches for his Father both above and below. When he can't find him in devotion, he looks for him in transgression.

I absorbed the meaning of these words gradually, like a bitter prescription, drop by drop, a tiny spoonful at a time. Whenever one of my brother's ideas flashed through my mind, my world was shaken. The chrysanthemums struggling against hot days and bitter nights threw caution to the winds and burst forth in a profusion of color with a great hurrah, as if thumbing their noses at the world.

I thought I, too, like the flowers, would be able to avoid the conflict taking place out in the world. All I had to do was to close the windows, lock the doors, and cover my head.

This was back when a house was a home, the home a universe, and human beings like planets circling around me, each with his own light, each influencing me in his own way. My young heart was still free of trodden paths. I was still absorbing impressions and etching them indelibly into my soul.

I sat by the window and watched as a spider that lived under our roof spun a palace out of nothing. She worked without stopping, with a passion, as if she were building a temple for all eternity. Why did she need a palace with such an intricate pattern? I wondered. Then I saw that the palace was really a trap, a net for ensnaring naïve insects and torturing them to death. She worked day and night, until the first winter storm washed away building and builder alike, along with the victims struggling in the web.

How fortunate I was, I thought, that my house was not built of cobwebs. The walls protected me from the wind, the roof from the rain. My father was snoring rhythmically by the oven; my stepmother was nursing the baby. Outside, snow was falling from a black sky, blanketing the ground with white. Gazing deep into the night, I mused that when my older brother found what he was looking for, he would come home and we would be happy once more. All the stars would encircle me. Anchored firmly in my world, I would rejoice that all was well.

As my thoughts wandered in this way, I heard someone fumbling at the door. I jumped out of bed and ran to let him in. But instead of my brother, it was the village errand boy, whose name I didn't know, who earned a few *groshns* carrying the birds from the rich people's homes to the slaughterhouse. If the chicken was a hen, the boy would grope in the right spot, and if there was an egg, he pulled it out and took it home as a gift for his mother.

"Your brother, ma'am," he stammered, "your brother has sent for you." I was surprised not so much by what he was saying as by how he addressed me.

"Do you need to see my brother, sir?" I said, responding with equal formality.

"No," he replied, "I don't need to see him. He needs to see me."

I gaped at him in the dim entryway. What nonsense was this? I left him standing there and ran back into the house. He followed me in. "Your brother," he repeated, more clearly this time, "they locked him up, but he got away. He's at Yankl the baker's house. He's naked, bare-foot, and all bloody, too."

My father awoke with a start: "What is he doing at the baker's?" he shouted at the boy. "Is he with that girl again?"

"Why are you picking on the boy?" my stepmother cried. "I knew that son of yours would bring disaster on us all. So he wanted to be a communist, eh? He was never satisfied. His life was too good for him."

"Shut your trap, woman," my father said. "Listen to me. You heard what the boy said — he's naked and barefoot, beaten black and blue." He sighed and bundled up a few things — my brother's old shoes, a shirt, a pair of pants.

"Go, take these," he said to me. "Me, I'm not going to the baker's house!" He pounded the table for emphasis.

We left together, the errand boy and I. We avoided the town, afraid someone would see us and alert the police, and instead set off for the river. It was frozen, but the new-fallen snow was not yet sticking to the surface and our footprints were not visible. We followed the river to the mill; the baker lived just beyond it.

My older brother looked small, broken, ashamed. His eyes were dim, his face red and swollen. He'd never made it over the border to where justice ruled. On this side of the border, the pogromists had knocked out two of his teeth. The thugs had stripped off his boots, his coat, and his pants and turned him over to the local police. A policeman threw him into a dark barn and ordered him to stay there while he went to look for something to cover his nakedness before delivering him to the commander.

Needless to say, my brother didn't wait for the policeman to return. He broke down the door and spent the next day hiding in a haystack. When night fell, naked and barefoot, he ran five kilometers to the baker's house.

There I found him sitting by the oven wrapped in a blanket. "Little Monkey!" he said in a broken voice. "You've grown into such a beauty!" As he spoke, he turned his head so I wouldn't see the tears in his eyes.

My brother liked to call me "Little Monkey," maybe because I enjoyed scrambling up trees. I'd never asked him why. How was I to address a person who was everything to me — father, mother, friend, beloved, perhaps even God? I lowered my gaze to the floor, leaving the question dangling in the air.

My brother stayed at the baker's house all winter. He spent his days in the attic. At night, he kneaded pans of bread. He heated the oven and from time to time stole a kiss from the baker's daughter, a small, pale girl, all skin and bones. During the day, little Skin-and-Bones would bring him food in the attic. The love that grew up between them was spontaneous, without design, oath, or contract, as natural as if it had just emerged from the Creator's workshop. Under the leaky roof, they built for themselves an Eden that lasted until spring.

Then someone suggested that he become a teacher in a nearby village, where the cause of justice had yet to find any takers. Any effort against the government was opposed by the citizens. There were no gendarmes, no police. Everyone was subject to the noble landowner's authority, and if anything displeased him, he would dispatch his hooligans, who knew all too well how to deal with rabble-rousers and restore order.

My brother was perhaps not handsome in the conventional sense. His beauty had to be sensed, as one senses the faintest note on a Stradivarius violin. When he spoke, his eyes lit up like golden suns captured in the prisms of a crystal chandelier. In order to grasp his beauty, one had to possess tracts of fallow earth that could receive the seeds that a strict father and a gentle mother had planted in his soul.

Throughout his lifetime this was my perception of him. I placed him on a pedestal composed not of stone or plaster but of pure fancy, without any imperfections whatsoever. After his death, he became the essential mythos that guided my psychic wanderings. For as long as he lived I could indulge in the luxury of being the flower that simply waits for the bee to do what she desires. . . .

Could it be that I never had a brother at all? Nor a home, a father and mother, a past? They say that an uneasy spirit can call up bizarre hallucinations. Am I myself nothing more than a hallucination, a nightmare passed down from generation to generation?

The other day I was sitting with my neighbor, chatting, as people do, about the other neighbors. Suddenly I had the feeling that I was speaking to a corpse. One moment my neighbor's shadow was dancing on the wall and the next moment it was stretched out on the ground. I asked her if she'd like a glass of tea. "Yes, I would," she said. I ran into the kitchen and put my head under running water. Knees knocking, I returned with the tea. My neighbor talked and laughed as if nothing had happened. The next day I learned she had died. I told no one about my premonition, considering it to be a personal matter. For such things they used to burn people at the stake. As for me, in this day and age I burn myself.

Well, so I created a brother in my imagination. I suppose I needed someone to lean on, someone upon whom I could build a foundation after the Holocaust.

I even imagined a love affair for him — not with the baker's simple daughter, but with a mermaid, a romantic nymph with golden braids and an enchanting laugh. I settled her at the edge of a pine forest, where a stream of pure water flowed to parts unknown. When she was still a child, the forest overseer had found the nymph beside the running stream. He'd taken her home and raised her as his own child.

My brother became acquainted with this lovely Musha, I imagined, when he ran away from the baker's attic and arrived in the village as a private tutor. She became his diligent student in matters of book learning and lovemaking alike. She loved to feel his passionate lips on her young body. She taught him the name of every blade of grass, every flower. She had a talent for hearing the first raindrop before it even hit the ground. She could spot the first swallow before the snow had begun to melt. And she grasped the trembling chord of my brother's heart and responded with the hot pulse of her young life.

Their meeting-place was a mound of sharp-scented pine needles under a canopy of branches. The forest, that great welcoming host, accepted them as it did all other living creatures. They did not need to keep any secrets from the forest, for whatever the forest saw it hid deep within itself. It sheltered the lovers and provided for the newly born and for all those housed in its domain. And it washed away the blood of the nighttime atrocities, so that when the sun rose anew, it heralded a truly new dawn.

On the night that the forest absorbed my brother's blood, Musha ran in search of her beloved. When she could not find him in the grotto, she went looking for him in the forest — first under the white linden tree and then underneath the birch. When night fell and he was still nowhere to be found, she huddled against the old oak. The squirrels nesting in its hollow trunk fled at her approach. A snake sprang out, then retreated. Musha felt for the crucifix around her neck but couldn't find it. She tried to scream, but her voice caught in her throat. The snake stretched out its head again and stared at the intruder in amazement. The maiden Musha didn't move a muscle; the two stared at each other as if hypnotized. Only when the snake withdrew did Musha raise her voice and call out to her lover. A black crow responded with a gruesome laugh. Musha believed that the crow was a premonition, a sign of certain death. The young thugs must surely have killed him. They had warned her to stop carrying on with the "kike." Now all became clear: it was a conspiracy, and her own father had had a hand in it, she realized. Just the other day he'd led her to the courtyard, saying the landowner's wife had a gift for her.

Musha hadn't wanted to go with him. On days when she had a rendezvous she liked to spend time singing and sunbathing in her flower garden. When the time for her date with my brother drew near, she would be suffused with the scents of the garden, the longing of her songs, the rays of the sun. This time, along with her charm, she brought him the gift presented to her by the landowner's wife: a red vest with silver trim. She wanted to surprise his fingers when they pressed into her breasts. . . . But now it was night, without stars or moon. The birds had stopped singing. Musha crouched beneath the oak as bats fluttered around her head and tangled in her hair. She raised her petticoat over her head. A deep exhaustion overcame her. She closed her eyes and dozed.

In her dream, white butterflies hovered in the air — quite a surprise at this time of year. Spring was still in its infancy. Seeds could be heard sprouting in the earth, and she could feel the spring within herself, too. Her breasts were delighted, straining against the laces of her red vest. The two undressed. His fingers, slender and pale, came toward her. Don't, my darling, don't touch, she said to him in her dream — a bridegroom must wait. . . . Look what a grand time the guests are having, see how they dance. They're rejoicing at our wedding, no matter what Father and Mother may say. . . .

Then the dream changed. Suddenly she was alone. People were running in all directions. The ribbons on her veil blocked her view. She could no longer see the guests, but only heard the commotion, which grew louder as it approached: children in the meadow chasing white butterflies and capturing them in glass jars. Suddenly a jar exploded. The shards flew all around; one landed on her chest. Musha opened her eyes to find the forest full of people — women running with flaming torches in their hands, men armed with axes, scythes, and poles. Everyone was laughing and shouting. A group surrounded her and called her a bitch, a Jew-whore. Someone grabbed her braids and dragged her out of her hiding-place. Another tore her vest. The tip of a boot pressed into her stomach. Someone spat in her face.

"So a kike took a liking to you?" screamed Katerina, their next-door neighbor. Musha knew that face; it had greeted her with a "good morning" every day of the year. It was the face of a woman, a mother — a friendly face, a human face. Now a witch stood before her, a Dionysian with round eyes glowing red like a crow's, with a flaming torch in hand. "Do you want to see him?" she screamed into Musha's face. "Look! He's hanging on the tree like a scarecrow!"

Musha did not turn her head. She didn't want to see his tortured body. For her he was still alive. For her, he would always continue to live as she had known him, as she had loved him. The crucifix she had reached for earlier now fell into her hands. She brought it to her lips. The crucified man on the tree and the one on the cross — both were

Jews. The realization shocked her, but also gave her courage. Musha straightened up, tightened her vest, smoothed her hair, and stepped away from the burning torches, the drunken laughter, and the crucified figure on the tree. She gathered it all into herself and grew still within an obstinate silence, as sharp and prickly as the needles of the pine forest.

A Snowstorm in Summerland

n winter, when New York is beset with ice and snow and plagued with blizzards, my husband starts up the old Ford, and like migratory birds we set out on our long journey from north to south.

Sitting idly in the passenger seat gives one the opportunity to think about many things. My husband does the driving so that we'll arrive in sunny Florida as quickly as possible. Meanwhile, I wonder why so many cars are heading north, toward the ice, the snow, the blizzards. I can't very well flag down a speeding automobile to ask, so I continue thinking. Questions that have no answers have a tendency to multiply, one thorny inquiry leading to a second, then a third. For no particular reason I find myself thinking about a friend of mine, a "progressive" person who has become a Lubavitcher Hasid.

Another friend has gone in the opposite direction and become a heretic. He claims he no longer believes in anything — not in God, not in man. Life, he says, is an illness, a contagious disease like the measles, passed on from one generation to the next. I let him talk, making no attempt to argue. It's important to him to have an exclusive claim on the truth. He suffered terribly during the Holocaust; I see him as a modern Job. No matter what he says, I nod my head. I can't win him over to my side, nor do I want to. Not that I have a side, of course. As a person, I am *pareve*, neutral, neither milk nor meat. I don't have the backbone necessary to win an argument, so I respect each person's opinions, no matter how bizarre they may be.

My friend the neo-Hasid, on the other hand, tries to hide behind a veil of privacy. He doesn't want to talk about the transformation of his soul — and that makes me want to press him for whys and wherefores. It can't be just because his first wife divorced him. He's much happier with the second wife, who gave him the son he'd been wanting for so many years. With the first wife he has two daughters, each prettier than the other. Beauty is not always a blessing, however. Like brains, it can be used for good or bad. For that matter, when it comes to good and bad, there are also differences of opinion. Conflicts have always existed, of course, but perhaps not at the current bewildering level. Today we live in a veritable Babylon, with no connection at all between parents and children.

My friend was upset when his older daughter, a student at an excellent college, came home for Yom Kippur and said she needed an abortion.

Her mother clutched her head in both hands.

"Stop yelling at me!" the daughter raged. "It was an accident!"

The crystal lamp over the holiday table suddenly went out. A shadow fell over the silver candlesticks.

"What do you mean, an accident?" the mother shouted.

"You know what I mean," the girl replied coldly.

"And if I do?" said the mother. "You want me to dance for joy?"

"Don't dance, don't make a scandal," the daughter said. "Just lend me two hundred dollars."

"Who's the father?" the mother asked. "Why aren't you getting married?"

"If I wanted to get married, I could," the daughter said. "I don't. I'm not becoming a mother at eighteen."

That evening my friend went to the synagogue and stayed until the very end of the Neilah prayer. Only the letters in the prayer book knew how agitated he was. Gazing into the book without saying a word brought him peace. The letters stared back at him with eyes of their own, eyes that had shed their own tears over sacred pages. They soothed his pain, took him by the hand, and showed him a new way forward along the ancient path.

The old Ford pushes on. The miles that had stretched before us are now far behind. Like a monster, the car gobbles up the minutes, hours, days, years. Could it be that it is Time that rushes past and I who stay in one place, trying to keep up? Knowing I have no say in the matter, I avoid looking at the speedometer, nor do I make any attempt to keep track of the time that is forever passing. Someone, I know, has taken care of this already, counting off so much and no more; at some point there will be none left. I drive these gloomy thoughts away. Why speculate about matters I don't understand? What can I do? Once things have been put in place, they're out of my hands. How does the old song put it? "And so the world turns." What will be will be, like it or not. In truth, though, I never stop struggling against fate, even if my resistance doesn't accomplish a thing. I started out with almost nothing, and what little I did inherit I tore to pieces with my bare hands. I unraveled the ancient tapestries, ripping apart the mysterious silhouettes thread by thread until I stood alone, outside the circle, waging war against myself.

The sky over the Carolinas is sheer blue. The cotton fields are empty. In one direction the landscape stretches to the horizon; on the other side, woods close in. In the gardens beside the squat little houses, lettuce is growing. A cow grazes in a pasture. Trees stand up to their knees in water. In some of the trees I see nests, all of them empty.

Who is it, I wonder, who maps the complex migrations of the birds?

It's chemistry, say the experts, and I suppose they must be believed. I can't ask the birds themselves, but I do wonder. I tend to assign human motivations to the animals that share our planet. I give myself license to judge which beast is intelligent and which bird beautiful. As a member of the human race in good standing, I grant myself a spot on the very highest rung, and until such time as I'm challenged by some other creature on the ladder, I'll stay up here and look down on all other beings.

I pay frequent visits to the Brooklyn Public Library, where I learn new things and also become aware of what I don't know. Along the way, I stop by the zoo. I hurry past the elephants, the lions, and the tigers and come to a halt in front of the monkey cage. I carry on a mute conversation with a golden-brown primate. Its sharp, clever eyes dart in all directions as it looks me over. The moment it fixes its stare on me, my attitude toward animals begins to dissolve. Long-forgotten gestures begin to assert themselves, fumbling for a language in which to communicate feelings without words. My fingertips tingle as if to reach out and touch the velvet fur, to comb the thick pelt for blood-sucking vermin. My eyes fill, the tears spill over, and I turn away, not wanting to infect my four-footed friend with my human complexes. Let it sit in its fenced-in paradise and wait for a free meal. Let it gobble the bananas tossed onto the floor and guzzle the water from the pump. Let it scamper up the ramps and believe them to be trees. Let it believe that today is forever — forever to live, forever to love, forever to believe that now is forever.

Resuming my trip to the library, I realize why Eve sought the company of the serpent. It's because she couldn't have a real conversation with Adam. All he would do was to obey his Creator's rules to the letter. No surprises from his quarter. So she turned to the snake, forfeiting the free meals in exchange for independence.

My pace slows. If it happened once, I think, it could certainly happen again — if not with a snake in the Garden of Eden, then perhaps with a creature from the farthest reaches of the galaxy. But there is no new thing under the sun, they say; what's been done will be done again. So maybe it will be the snake again after all, in its original form, before it lost its hands and feet, its power of speech, its keen intelligence and its will.

The question arises: How will the two of us communicate, my snake and I? On television, all the aliens speak English, which is all well and good, but mine might speak Swahili, or the language of birds or beasts, or the voice of the wind or the roar of the sea. When my snake comes, will we confine it in a cage? Put it in the circus?

I walk on, my shadow following like a puppy. Shadows fascinate me; they remind me of something forgotten. For me, a shadow is not as abstraction without substance, but the image in a block of stone, the word in thought before it comes to expression.

Entering the library, I forget about such speculations. I select two romantic novels, *Anna Karenina* and *Madame Bovary*. I'm eager to look again at what these women gained, what I've given up. Maybe I want to console myself with the notion that things are not so bad inside my self-made prison. Yet even in this day and age, tearing down bars is a heroic act. When Ibsen's Nora walked out and slammed the door on her marriage, the echo was heard around the world. But as for how the world treated Nora afterwards — that the playwright did not say.

Absorbed in my own adventures, I fail to notice when we cross from one state into another. The sky looks the same, and so does the earth — but no, here in Georgia the earth is redder, and the sky that was clear and blue on the other side of the border is suddenly heavy with clouds. The cawing of crows fills the air, and the horizon is engulfed by a black forest. I see a dead horse lying beside a culvert. A single snowflake lands on the windshield, then another, and before I know it the whiteness is flying in all directions, descending over the landscape like the traditional veiling of the bride.

"What are you doing, writing poetry?" my husband asks, irritated. While he drives, I'm supposed to be watching out for changes in the weather. This is my job, or should be, according to the rules of logic. But in my case logic is on vacation.

Meanwhile, the snow continues to fall in a most un-Southern fashion. The young man who filled the gas tank a while back warned that a storm was headed our way, but we didn't believe him. The sky was as fair as a fresh-laid egg and the sun so strong I had to lower the visor on my window. From the mirror on the visor a pale face comes swimming out to meet me, its hair disheveled, its wrinkles displaying without mercy what I'm at pains to conceal. The face reminds me of Aunt Rokhl, who looked like this as she sat by the window and gazed out onto Prospect Park, expressing her philosophy of life in the sing-song melody of the Jewish woman's Bible: "Behold, my child, how everything on God's earth refreshes itself. The trees do bloom and the grass doth grow, but man doth wilt and his limbs do wither. He giveth up his soul to his Creator and his body to the dust from which it came."

Death, for me, summons up more shame than fear. I was ashamed when my mother died — ashamed for her sake, ashamed for life itself which is condemned to die. How could a person in the prime of life simply drop dead? She had decided to travel to the famous spa in Krynica, had a blue suit made, bought a new hat with feathers and an umbrella with red cherries on the handle. After she died, the suit and the umbrella were stored in a trunk, the hat with feathers wrapped in tissue paper in the depths of the closet. The hat and the umbrella, especially its red cherries, filled me with shame.

I turn up the visor with its mirror. No, I will not accept the inevitable. Not yet. In my dreams and in reality, I'm still who I used to be. And after a week of sun and swimming in the mild sea water, my wrinkles will disappear and my color will be restored. I'll be able to fool the world and maybe even myself.

"Are you asleep?" my husband demands. He's out of patience. "Can't you tell the difference between a car trip and one of your silly little poems? A car can't figure out where it's going by magic, you know. Do you have the slightest idea where we are? Where is the Howard Johnson's? Where's the Holiday Inn? If you weren't so busy daydreaming, you would have seen the signs. Now we're totally lost."

My husband believes he has a right to control my thoughts. He belongs to the old school, in which everything functions as a system, and the slightest deviation from the established order means a loss of control over himself and others. Knowing how upset he is, I say nothing. I search in vain for the orange roof of a Howard Johnson's, which can usually be seen from miles away. Night is falling, the snow is whirling, and the car skids on the slippery road as my husband takes out his rage on the gas pedal. He presses down harder, and the car seems to take off in flight. The cars in front of us and those coming toward us are invisible. Suddenly we hear the shriek of a siren. Are they after us? My husband eases up on the gas and the old Ford slides to a stop. The siren's whine approaches, then cuts off beside us. A policeman knocks on the window and politely asks to see a driver's license. Anxiously we await his verdict. But it's not up to him to settle the matter, he says. For driving 80 miles an hour, we have to go before the sheriff.

We turn around and head back where we came from. The policeman leads the way. The revolving beams of his car light up the road ahead. The white fields and the snowflakes made golden by the headlights are as strange and fantastic as a scene in a story book. After two long, monotonous days of sitting in the car and staring at the unchanging landscape, even a policeman on a stormy night is a welcome diversion. Maybe it's a good thing. But no, my thoughts begin to spin as wildly as the storm outside the window. What if the courteous officer is actually a bandit who has stolen the police car? What if he's planning to rob us, or worse? Such things have been known to happen. I see no sign of human habitation. He could be leading us to a godforsaken spot to carry out something too terrible to think about. By the flashing light I see that my husband has turned pale. I don't dare ask if he, too, suspects the worst.

I imagine him leading us into the woods and ordering us out of the car. He points a loaded revolver and makes us empty our pockets, hand over jewelry and cash. He takes the registration papers and turns the Ford over to his partner, who's been crouching in the police car all along. They take off with both cars and leave us behind in the woods.

Well, I think, that wouldn't be so bad. It could be worse.

Worse in what way? I ask myself. Robbed and abandoned in a dark wood without shelter or warm clothing, me in open-toed shoes and a light jacket, my husband also in his summer clothes. . . .

On the other hand, one night in the woods won't kill us. It will allow us to taste, if only in the tiniest way, what our brothers and sisters experienced in another era.

Absorbed in the horrors of that tragic time, I find myself disappointed when we emerge from the woods. Light floods in from all directions. Screaming neon signs announce the presence of the Howard Johnson's and the Holiday Inn. The policeman leads us to a one-story building with a title on the door: John Macmillan, Sheriff.

We get off with a fifty-dollar fine.

"You see," says my husband, now completely calm, "everything works out for the best. Who knows what disaster that policeman saved us from? We could have crashed into a tree, or been struck from behind. In such a blizzard, God only knows what could have happened."

And now here we are at the Holiday Inn, in a spacious room with a clean bathtub and hot water. The bed is made up with white pillows and woolen blankets. Under the pink lampshade on the night table, two candies are waiting to gladden the heart. Reluctant to enjoy these good things, I stand at the window. I see the distant forest from which there was no escape. I see the faces of loved ones and of strangers. I want to bow my head to the ground and beg forgiveness from all the bones that were denied a proper burial.

For a long time, I stand at the window lost in thought.

YOSEMITE PARK

On the trip to Yosemite Park, along with my curiosity I brought a pair of binoculars, a warm coat, some candy for energy, and the inevitable camera. I'd left my pen and notebook on the table in the hotel, but this was no catastrophe, I told myself. Thousands of other people had already written, painted, sung, philosophized, and sculpted their reactions to the magnificent waterfall. What did I have to add? The point was simply to see with my own eyes, to absorb with my senses the wonder of God's world.

Two days earlier, I'd visited the Grand Canyon. As I gazed into the abyss, the rubble-strewn chaos looked like New York after an atomic blast. I could see the tower of the Empire State Building at rest in the dry riverbed where the Hudson had flowed. Sculptures from the Metropolitan Museum of Art lay smashed among the ruins of Rockefeller Center. Searching for traces of Central Park, I spotted an old woman seated on a stone bench. In the depths of the East River, the treasures of Wall Street lay scattered to the four winds — gold ingots glittering

among piles of bird excrement. I sensed despair in the granite faces
staring up at me with mice running in and out of their gaping
mouths. Only the lions of the 42nd Street Library seemed in their
element, as robust as ever, smiling in satisfaction. As if in a trance, I
took in the scene, a glimpse into the future from which there was no
escaping, no hiding, no staying away — like a vision just before death.

Later I bought some picture postcards. The bus was waiting; I was
the last one on board. I settled into my seat and leaned my head against
the window. The blazing sunset burned into the abyss and the faint
echo of a distant ram's horn sounded in my ears: *yisgadal ve-yiskadash*,
"Magnified and sanctified be Your great name" — the opening of the
Kaddish, the prayer for the dead. As darkness fell, the bus hurried on
into the night. I closed my eyes and imagined the dinner awaiting me
at the hotel.

Traveling with a group has its pros and cons. There's no need to
keep an eye on the speedometer or worry about where to spend the
night — the driver takes care of everything. It's all pre-arranged, down
to the minute, but that means you can't sleep late or stop when something interests you. At lunchtime, I usually sit apart from the group.
It's not that I think I'm better than they are. Far from it. I know that
because of my limited social skills I'm missing the interesting conver-
sations along with the boring ones. Still, I go off by myself, if only a
few steps away from the professional prattlers. What I experience on
my own stays with me. If I'm not able to recall a memory at will,
eventually it comes back to me on its own terms. Sometimes a pres-
ent-day experience becomes entangled with a long-forgotten event
that once affected me. When past and present meet, the flash of the
collision lights up the vanished era in full color.

On the way to Yosemite, we stopped to see the sequoia trees, the
so-called monarchs of the forest — the oldest living things on God's
earth. Even the chatterboxes fell silent as we beheld these colossal

giants, 300 feet high and 4,000 years old. A sense of awe overtook us as we stood before them. No one uttered a word. Had Adam and Eve coupled in their shadows? How long would they remain like this, rooted in eternity? Would man with his machines kill them off? Such were the thoughts that crept into my mind as the bus lumbered up the narrow trail through the Mariposa Grove, where the trees blocked out the sun. No sign of civilization — everything as it was at the dawn of creation.

It was late afternoon by the time we arrived at Yosemite and walked to the fantastic site called Bridal Veil, where a waterfall descends from a worn granite mountainside more than 1400 feet tall. "Some bride!" a woman with blond hair and a wrinkled face exclaimed. "No wonder she's still a virgin! What man could satisfy such a creature?"

I moved away from the group and sat down in the long grass with my face to the wall. From underneath the ruins of time a bride stepped forth, a refined young woman with flaming red hair. Her tiny face was round, pale, expressionless. Wearing a floor-length veil, a gift from Aunt Bashe, she was being led to the cemetery, where she was to be married to the town bathhouse attendant, a widower with three small children. The fifty years between then and now fell away. I could see Aunt Bashe with her formidable bulk, a beautiful woman who in her youth, despite being penniless, had managed to marry the wealthy heir to a dry goods store. After the two had been together for several years, people began to say Bashe was barren. She rejected the idea out of hand. "Barren?" she scoffed. "In the Bible, Sarah was ninety years old when she made them eat their ugly words" — and she herself was still young.

Aunt Bashe lived in the days of horse and wagon, but she had a mouth like an express train. When a customer came in for a simple swatch of linen, she could talk him into a deal on a remnant for a suit, a bit of batiste for his wife, and a length of velvet for his sons' trousers. If he was short of cash, no matter. She knew her customers, sensed who could be trusted to pay and who could not.

People said Aunt Bashe had struck gold with her husband. True, he was spoiled, shallow, and not especially attractive or intelligent, but he had the great advantage of being easy to manipulate.

One day, as the Sabbath was coming to a close, the couple sat down for the evening meal. The candles mirrored the gold of the setting sun. Light shimmered on the eastern wall like a school of fish swimming silently and sedately across the room until the end of time.

The maid had just brought in the gefilte fish, the wine and the challah. Aunt Bashe looked at the wall awash in goldfish, then turned to her husband. "I've tried all the old wives' remedies," she said. "Now it's up to you, my dear. You see our maid — she's as naïve as a chick just out of the egg. Have your way with her. Do it tonight. If it was good enough for Abraham, it's good enough for us."

Srul-Vulf gripped his head in both hands. "Me? Take advantage of an innocent orphan girl? Heaven help us!"

"Take advantage?" Bashe replied. "We'll be doing her a favor. After she bears us a child to raise as our own, God willing, we'll marry her off and she can have children by her lawful husband. And maybe," she went on, "thanks to her good deed my own womb will open — something our holy foremothers knew about, even if today's women don't."

"But how will you manage it?" asked Srul-Vulf, his beard curling up like a question mark. "People have eyes. A pregnant girl can't hide her belly."

"Leave it to me," answered Aunt Bashe. "Go to her like Abraham to the servant Hagar, like Jacob to the servant Zilpah. I'll take care of the rest."

This is what was said that Sabbath night, or words to that effect, and this is what was done. After the fish and the wine, Srul-Vulf knocked at the maid's room. The girl had already gone to bed. She came to the door in a short nightgown, her breasts uncovered. The sight of her employer filled her with terror. She ran back to bed and pulled the covers over her head. Srul-Vulf blew out the lamp and felt his way to her in the dark.

When the girl began to show, Aunt Bashe hired a horse and wagon, settled her into the straw, and sent her away to a sister who ran an inn in a neighboring village. Bashe outfitted herself with a pillow under her petticoat. The pillow grew bigger and bigger — a poke in the eyes of the spiteful townspeople. When the time came, she went to the village and returned with a son bundled up in the very same pillow.

Summer arrived, and winter, and then came a summer of great abundance. In the marketplace, sellers sang out the cheap prices of the fruits that filled their stalls. Children played in the streets and laughed at the world, their faces smeared with black cherries. Then, suddenly, there came a plague. Little children dropped like flies. Every day an alarm was sounded to summon the residents for instructions about boiling their water and washing their hands before meals. The delicious cherries were doused with kerosene while the venders wrung their hands, hurled oaths at the police, and pleaded with God to call off the plague.

One day during these darkest of times, it was decided — maybe in hopes that the ceremony would drive out the plague, as was the belief, or maybe not — to erect a wedding canopy in the cemetery and marry off Aunt Bashe's maid to the bathhouse attendant. The event excited the entire town. Young and old escorted the bride up the hill to the holy place. Exactly how the match would end the plague, no one knew. No one asked why the poor maid was to be wed to the old widower with three children, or why the ceremony had to take place at the cemetery. But the very peculiarity of the match was enough to convince people that it might bring forth a miracle.

The most important men in town carried the poles of the wedding canopy. Aunt Bashe, her head covered with a holiday scarf, led the bride by the arm. From my perch on my father's shoulders, I could see her being taken to the half-sunken gravestones of her parents. A woman prayer-leader with a kerchief pulled down over her forehead was whispering to her. But the bride's lips were sealed. She rocked back and forth, shoulders shuddering, not a sound emerging from her mouth. The wind played with her veil and her long dress.

Under the canopy, the groom waited in his black coat and broad-brimmed hat. Two of his grown children stood by his side. Across from them, a man with a white beard was swaying back and forth, his eyes in his holy book. Aunt Bashe brought the bride to the canopy. There stood the gravedigger, a follower of the rabbi whose merits would help bring an end to the plague, with a dead baby in his arms. Beside him was a musician with a fiddle. Both were waiting for a sign. The old man with the white beard began to say a prayer under his breath. Aunt Bashe wiped her eyes. The bride's eyes were dry. The groom took her hand, but he couldn't find the ring. As he fumbled through his pockets, the bride acted as if the whole scene had nothing to do with her. Her eyes were fixed on the single ray of sunshine that was breaking through the heavy clouds high over the groom's entourage, over his broad-brimmed black hat, over the man with the white beard, over the fiddler and the gravedigger holding the dead child. She spoke with closed lips, her eyes smiling. Suddenly the skies burst open. A bolt of lightning parted the heavenly bridal veil. Like a spear aimed by an unseen hand, it passed over the forest and skipped over the river and the walls surrounding the cemetery. When it reached the wedding canopy, the bride fell dead to the ground.

A tremendous commotion ensued. The crowd stampeded down the hill, pursued by thunder and lightning. I clung to my father's neck. The dead bride seemed to be following us, flying overhead with her long veil tangled in a white cloud that hung down to the ground. A ram's horn sounded, congratulating the newlyweds. Then a voice from the heavens could be heard to speak the blessing of bereavement: "Blessed is the True Judge!"

The driver's horn was sounding. I stood up. Dusk had fallen. Birds were swooping through the air, cars crowding toward the exit. In my imagination I could still see the wedding at the cemetery in all its mysterious splendor. Etched forever in my memory, the picture had endured intact for a full fifty years. Unlike the enchanted princess who was awakened by the kiss of a prince, Aunt Bashe's maid knew nothing of princes. Perhaps when she drew water from the well she sometimes looked down into the depths and shed a tear or two. And perhaps these tears ascended from the well into the clouds, where they mingled with the tears of all the incinerated brides that rose with the smoke from the chimneys of Auschwitz. Thus joined together, they drifted over sea and shore, suspended in the veil of eternity.

PASTORALE

The poet may claim that "April is the cruelest month," but for me the cruelest of all is October. In October we turn back the clock and the days grow shorter, the nights longer. Winter waits by the door, sharpening its teeth. Soon it will bite into the innocent pansies and proud chrysanthemums, hunt down the late-blooming rose bush that clings to the wall and crush it into the mud. Meanwhile the flowers keep on flirting with the pale sun, soaking up the rays as if imbibing an elixir of eternal youth. Absorbed in their personal Song of Songs, they're unaware of the beginning of the end. They don't see the falling leaves, the trees stripped bare, the unavoidable fate that looms ahead.

On autumn mornings, the sun is in no rush to cast off its night-clothes, nor am I. In summer I leap out of bed ready to take on the world. Now I linger under the covers thinking of everything and nothing. A friend of mine once said that thinking was a loafer's invention. Back then I didn't have time for thinking, so I allowed the words to sink into my reservoir of memory, along with other clever (or foolish) sayings I had put aside for my retirement.

My husband is the first to get out of bed. Rather than giving in to idle thoughts, he summons his manly pride like a shield to protect himself from danger. He bathes, shaves, and pulls on work pants as if he's planning to build a house. The leaves that have fallen overnight are waiting for him, and so are the birds. He pours out their grain and takes pleasure in observing them at their meal. He presides like the lord of the manor, allowing no quarrels. When his work is done, he retrieves the morning paper from the doorstep, comes inside, and spreads it out before him, a contented smile gracing the smooth planes of his face.

It takes me longer to get moving on these autumn mornings. Not until I smell fresh-brewed coffee do I put on my faded robe and stuff my feet into well-worn slippers. My husband takes a look at my tousled hair and wrinkled face and shakes his head. I can tell he doesn't like looking at what's become of me, but I distract him with a "good morning." "Good morning," he answers, nose in the paper. He grumbles over the reporters — sensationalists who will do anything to advance their reputations.

When I don't respond, he gets up and goes to his room with the stock market pages, leaving the rest of the paper on the table.

After my second cup of coffee, I feel a surge of energy. I remember the two stray cats that are counting on me for their rations. If I'm even slightly late with their bowl, they make a meal of the birds. Sometimes they kill not out of hunger but for sport. They pierce the victim's throat and lay the corpse on my doorstep.

I've asked my husband to stop feeding the birds. In return for the small amount of food he gives them, they suffer heavy losses. He replies that I should stop feeding the cats. What right does a person have to interfere in the affairs of the animal world? he asks. If man can't even stop killing his fellow man, why get involved in the conflicts of other species?

The problem is, he's always right. Arguing with him only depresses me, so I try to avoid it. On sunny days, I stretch out on my chaise longue and watch as he gathers up the broken branches and stacks them neatly under the terrace awning. Why so many branches? I wonder. He already has enough for ten winters. Has he forgotten about the growth on the left side of his brain? The doctor says an operation is not necessary. A tumor such as this could stay the same for years, he says. There's no guarantee, though. "We don't know what keeps it stable," the doctor says. "It could wake up without warning and start to spread, and we wouldn't be able to do anything to stop it."

"Haven't you done enough?" I ask my husband. "Go change your clothes. It's shabbas."

"So?" he answers. "The wheels stop turning on shabbas?"

Yes, I think, for some they do, but I say nothing. I observe the steady stream of young couples dressed in their Sabbath best on their way to the synagogue. Some have children with them, boys with the traditional sidelocks and yarmulkes and girls with colorful ribbons in their hair. Twenty or thirty years ago, when we were young, it was the old people who went to services while the young ones stayed home to wash their cars, paint their houses, work in their gardens. Back then the ones who went to services were seen as a doomed lot. Today the wheel has turned. The old people work in their gardens while the young are drawn to the ancient well. "One cannot live by bread alone," I think as I watch them pass.

For me, shabbas is the saddest day of the week, full of uninvited memories. A Jew with a long beard walks by — and I see my father, bathed in the light of the Sabbath soul that relieves him from weekday cares. On shabbas even poverty is transformed. The table is set, the floor freshly washed in preparation for the Sabbath bride. Intoxicated by the smell of poppy seed cakes, I polish the candlestick with its three branches. The face staring back at me from the shiny surface contains the secret of my tomorrows. One moment I'm a princess, the next moment a freak.

"Enough with the rubbing!" my mother scolds. "You're taking off all the silver. Any more and the tin will show through."

Rubbing off the surface shine — such has been my tendency all my life. I've done it with my husband, my children. Maybe I'd be doing it still, if not for the bugaboo lurking in my husband's brain. "Avoid excitement," the doctor says. "Leave him alone. Try not to upset him." I obey these instructions to the letter. Instead of upsetting him, I do the worrying myself. Why has it been more than four weeks since our son called? Why did our daughter divorce her Jewish husband and run off with a gentile?

"Who were you talking to on the phone?" my husband asks.

"Our daughter," I answer casually, as if I talk to her all the time.

"I thought you weren't on speaking terms," he says.

"How long can you stay angry at your own daughter?"

"Well then," he asks, "did you ask her if she's planning to start a family?"

"Mothers don't ask such questions these days," I answer. "They listen and keep their mouths shut."

He thrusts his hands into his pants pockets and rummages as if searching for an answer. Meanwhile he paces around the room, and when he can't find a way out he comes to a stop and looks at me. "I know a man, a rich man," he says, "who in such a case willed his estate to a yeshiva."

"Your child is still your child," I answer. "Maybe we contributed to the error of her ways." Maybe we failed to set a good example. In any case, it's too late now. She seems happy, so we, too, must be happy.

I often think we should get a dog. Or if not a dog, then a cat or a bird. A living creature with its own take on right and wrong. I could talk to a cat without fear of distressing her. I could tell her I live in the shadow of death and her facial expression wouldn't change in the slightest. She would lie quietly in my lap and allow herself to be stroked. My words would put her to sleep. She would breathe rhythmically, like an integral part of eternity. If I were a cat, I'd do the same. I'd lay my head in a warm lap and dream.

When the north wind begins to whistle angrily over all of creation, I get out my ball of yarn and my knitting needles. Years ago, I intended to turn the ball of yarn into a sweater for my son, but he got married and I forgot about the project. Now I'm knitting a sweater for my husband. I'm in no hurry. An unbidden voice whispers that I should take my time. As long as I knit, I hold the Angel of Death at bay. So I do as the Greek Penelope did, Odysseus's wife — I knit by day and unravel by night.

A delusion is worse than a disease, my father used to say. I've deluded myself into believing that finishing the sweater means signing my husband's death sentence.

My husband is still busy with the stocks and bonds. He says he's trying to figure out whether we can afford a winter in Florida without drawing down our principal. I'm not sure he means what he says, though. I suspect that, like me, he's wrestling with his own premonitions — he in his room and I in the kitchen. A certain intimacy prevails in the kitchen. The boiling kettle fills the room with steam. Time was when four of us ate together at the table. Then three. Beyond that I don't want to think. I hold the sweater in my lap without knitting. The telephone is silent. The wind whistles. The first snow has fallen and Hanukkah arrives. The candles are burning and my husband is running a fever. He recites the blessing over the candles and goes back to bed. The doctor says he has the flu and needs a good chicken soup. I do as the doctor orders, but the fever comes and goes.

"How's the sweater coming along?" my husband asks gruffly. I knit faster, until the sweater is big enough to fit. And although we both laugh, my heart beats faster. Unseen hands are pointing their skinny fingers. The doctor says the flu has returned. He must go to the hospital for a comprehensive examination. Whenever the doctor addresses my husband he smiles from ear to ear. He claps my husband on the back and speaks heartily. On the other side of the door, his smile is nowhere to be found.

He never comes home from the hospital. Spring arrives, and summer and autumn. Yellow leaves fall from the trees. No one collects them. The wind lifts them and sends them in eddies out to the street, where the speeding cars grind them into dust. I debate within myself: should I rake them up the way he used to do and turn the pile into a bed for the cats in the alley? Or should I leave them in God's care? Should I make something to eat? Should I crack the covers of a book? Yes, the golden sunsets still move me as always. I get up off the sagging couch and go out to meet them. I walk up and down along the beach and greet other widows. I don't know these women, but I recognize myself in the halo of diminution that widowhood together with the years has woven around our heads. Dressed in black, I go often to the old age home. Once a week I read aloud from Isaac Bashevis Singer's *Stories from Behind the Stove* in Yiddish. After I read, the audience peppers me with questions having nothing to do with the book. A woman with only one tooth wants to know if God exists. Another answers that simply by voicing such a question she's causing the Messiah to tarry.

Within the residents of the old age home, the spark of Jewishness still glows. They're not shy about expressing themselves. One woman sitting at the window tries to catch a fly that buzzes by. . . . When she succeeds, she carefully raises the sash and releases it into the world.

"Maybe a gentle breeze will carry it off into a field of flowers," she says, "and there it will live out its life in joy and satisfaction."

"Don't be ridiculous!" cries a bleached blonde in a hot red blouse. "Such a fuss over a fly!"

The woman who has freed the fly doesn't reply. She stands up and leaves the room. I follow her with my eyes. There is something aristocratic in her bearing, her smooth white hair and her pale face. Her eyes express a certain sadness, as if to say that we understand each other.

The next time I come, the woman is no longer there. She has thrown herself out of a fifth-floor window.

Not so long ago, I reflect, these old people were little children pressed tenderly to their mothers' bosoms. All too soon they were mothers and fathers themselves. Now they tremble like dry leaves on the bough, faces clouded, eyes dim, counting the hours from one meal to the next. Is this what the future holds for me? A chill runs down my spine. I approach the man who always acts the know-it-all — an interesting person who usually sits at the head of the group with his back to the window, pronouncing judgment on religious matters. He can talk rings around anyone. Now, with the fervent sing-song of a Lubavitcher Hasid, he's quoting from a chapter of the Psalms. He has the group in the palm of his hand. No one asks questions. He doesn't like to be put on the spot, preferring to supply both questions and answers himself. His specialty is arguing with God. If someone does dare to ask a question, he invokes the Ruler of the Universe who thought the whole thing up in the first place. "Imagine," he says — "if man with his limited years on earth can get tired of the game, how must it feel to live forever? The Almighty got sick of spinning around and around a long time ago. He washed his hands of us and went off to build a better world."

When I read aloud, he falls asleep — or seems to, anyway. I have a feeling he's actually paying attention but can't bring himself to descend from his hard-won perch. Sitting and listening to a woman read *Stories from Behind the Stove* makes him feel like a horse among cows. Although he keeps his past under lock and key, the number on his arm reveals his secret. Sometimes, when the spirit moves him, he sings selections from the Yiddish theater. He knows the names of all the dead actors. Those who are among the living he dismisses with a wave of the hand.

THE FATE OF THE YIDDISH WRITER

I am a housewife, a wife, a mother, a grandmother — and a Yiddish writer. I write my stories in Yiddish. Yiddish is in my bones. When I hear my mother's "Oy!" in my head, I lift my eyes to the heavens and hear God answering me in Yiddish. The birds, real and imagined, speak Yiddish, and the wind at my window speaks Yiddish — because I speak Yiddish, think in Yiddish. My father and mother, my sisters and brothers, my murdered people seek revenge in Yiddish. No world language is comparable to Yiddish, with its unique sighs, its unmatched sense of humor.

After the melody has died away and the tears have ebbed, there remains an echo that travels on the wind. Do not wipe out the language that accompanied your people to the mass grave, the echo says. Do not take up the murderers' sword with your own hand. Do not allow the word that bloomed in bitter climes to wither. Remember Amalek. Remember Hitler. Do not extinguish the spark that smolders in the ashes. Those who deny the past can have no future. Remember!

So here I sit, writing from right to left. My older brother watches over me, telling me what to write in Yiddish. I can't very well ask him not to speak in the language of exile. Blessed with the gifts of a prodigy, he knows what I'm thinking. Yiddish is not a language of exile, he answers my unspoken words — it is *mame-loshn*, our mother tongue.

I have tremendous respect for my brother. He believed in the goodness of man, the goodness of all. He met with a double disaster — disappointed first in his faith, then in himself. Now he watches over me, directing my stories from beyond the grave with a sure touch. This is how it was. This is what happened. So must it be recorded. Each according to his ability must convey what he saw, what he lived through, what he thought, what he felt. You did not survive simply to eat blintzes with sour cream. You survived to bring back those who were annihilated. You must speak in their tongue, point with their fingers. . . .

I sit and I write, page after page, covering reams with my handwriting. In truth, I'm sorry to part with these pages full of the tears and laughter of my girlfriends and the boys they fell in love with — all in Yiddish. I'm sorry to let go of the men in their kaftans and the women they quarreled and made up with — always in Yiddish. I'm sorry to send off the cozy sounds and colors that imbued Jewish life with such beauty and charm back then, reluctant to send them away across the ocean to a place where Yiddish is seen as a source of embarrassment. The very language that nurtured the Zionist dream and brought it to fruition is now untouchable in that land. But since I belong to this people that spits in its own face, I pack up my manuscript and send it off — to Israel.

I'm not expecting to become rich or famous. My reward is the writing itself, the putting down on paper of that which will not leave me in peace. Above all I don't want to forsake my brother and end up isolated and alone in my own home.

Meanwhile, I sit and wait for an answer. I wait as if my writing were entirely dependent on the publisher's yes or no. While I'm waiting, the muse abandons me. After assembling some 300 pages, I want to know what the experts have to say. But it turns out the experts don't actually read the manuscript. All they do is count the pages and send the author a bill for the publishing. So many sheets amount to a five followed by three fat zeroes. To proofread the galleys and illustrate the title page raises the price by one followed by another three zeroes. They politely ask for half the total as soon as possible to enable them to continue their work.

Faced with collecting such a fantastic sum of money, the masochist in me takes charge, reminding me that I have in my possession a gold chain and a sparkling diamond ring and pointing out that I could get along perfectly well without such vanities. It tells me where to sell the jewelry. Just listen to the radio, it says; the announcer will provide the address. I put down my writing tools and do as I'm told. As soon as I've sent the check, I return to my desk. But instead of picking up my pen, I take my head in my hands and rock like a mourner after a funeral.

When I open my eyes, I see my brother's shadow on the wall, rocking back and forth like me. Dry leaves are playing with the wind. The summer birds have packed up and flown away. The wild geese remain behind, feeding by the lake. On the bare winter branches, tiny gray birds are sitting and waiting for bread crumbs. I, too, am waiting, for the next letter from the publisher.

It arrives the week before Passover. At first I don't allow myself to open the envelope — God only knows what lies within, good or bad. Years of work hang in the balance. Finally, here it is, short and sweet. About the work itself, not a word. But at least I've achieved one thing: the letter addresses me as "Esteemed Writer," which means, I suppose, that it's official — from now on I'm a writer. I read on: You are of course aware of the difficult situation in our country. Inflation is on the rise. A pair of pants that yesterday went for $10 now costs twice as much. Of course you will understand that we cannot proceed at the earlier price. To be fair to both sides, we are asking for just $1,000 more. Please be so kind as to send the check immediately and we will finish the work right away.

Ashamed, insulted, depressed, I begin to compose an answer. Surely a press with a world reputation is more than a two-bit businessman haggling over a sack of oakum? We're talking about a book — a book full of living characters. It occurs to me to choose a work by some dead author and retype the text word for word — then sign my name and see if they'd even notice.

I stand there with the letter in my hand, considering. Which will it be? Should I run to the bank for a $1,000 check? Or pick a volume off my shelf and start typing? My resentment grows. In tears, I go to the telephone and call a close friend, a well-known poet. I pour out my bitter heart.

"What are you talking about?" he says in response to my agitated words. "Where have you been? Don't you understand how our literary racket works? Wait until the book is out in print — then you'll really see what it means to be a writer among Jews. I hate to say it, but unless you want your books to gather dust in the cellar, you're going to have to roll up your sleeves and distribute them yourself."

"But where?" I ask, dumbfounded. "How?"

"Well you may ask," he says. "You'll learn to beg addresses from friends and acquaintances. Some will send you a few dollars and others won't. But first, my dear, you'll do what old Noah did: you'll send your book out into the world like the dove from the ark and you'll wait for the critics to respond. Yes, my friend, it's not easy. But there's no way around it. For Yiddish writers like us, such is fate."

Translators' Acknowledgments

Our first debt is to Paul Lempel, who not only granted permission to translate Blume Lempel's work, but also shared his memories and provided access to her correspondence. Several other family members were also kind enough to share their memories with us.

We thank Robert Mandel of Mandel Vilar Press and Merrill Leffler of Dryad Press for their enthusiasm and their vision. They have truly been a pleasure to work with. Thanks, too, to Sandy Rodgers of Dryad Press and to Fran Forman for her cover art.

Our project would not have begun without the encouragement of David Roskies. Norman Buder was extraordinarily generous with his time in sharing his tremendous knowledge of Yiddish and *yidishkayt*.

We are grateful to the Hadassah-Brandeis Institute and the Sonya Staff Foundation for vital financial support. Debby Olins at the Hadassah-Brandeis Institute graciously responded to our queries.

Thanks are due to the Yiddish Book Center for awarding the 2012 Translation Prize to our work and for publishing early versions of two translations.

Marc Caplan, Brukhe Lang Caplan, Kathryn Hellerstein, Anita Norich, Jeffrey Shandler, and Sheva Zucker offered valuable insights from their expertise as Yiddish translators and scholars. Pearl Gluck, Cecile Kuznitz, and Roberta Newman vigorously encouraged our work. Yitskhok Niborski and Roger Kohn assisted with French linguistic issues and the French cultural context.

Itzik Gottesman provided us with a videotape of his 1985 interview of Lempel, which enabled us to see and hear the author on film, sitting in her back yard, talking and reading from her work. Troim Katz Handler shared her memories and provided us with cassette tapes and a transcript of a visit that she and a group of Yiddish cultural activists paid to Lempel in 1992. Julia Mazow, herself a translator of Blume Lempel's work, shared correspondence and memories of Lempel. Alexander Spiegelblatt shared letters from Blume Lempel and memories of publishing her work in *Di goldene keyt*.

Sharon Horowitz and Rachel Becker of the Hebraic Section of the Library of Congress and Lyudmila Sholokhova of the Library of the YIVO Institute for Jewish Research responded to research queries and provided materials that were vital for our work.

Our Yiddish reading group enthusiastically supported our project. We thank Morris Faierstein, Jim Feldman, Miriam Isaacs, the late Motl Rosenbush, Harvey Spiro, Jonathan Sunshine, Henrietta Wexler, and Natalie Wexler. And thanks to Jeff Blum for graciously surrendering the dining room table on many Sunday afternoons and for his counsel and support.

Ellen would like to acknowledge the late Max Rosenfeld, a beloved teacher who ushered her into the world of Yiddish when she began studying the language as a memorial to her mother. Max bestowed his own copy of Lempel's *A rege fun emes*, inscribed with the author's compliments.

A word on the translation process: the two of us came to the project with different approaches to language and literature, which worked to our advantage over the several years we spent together inside the world of Blume Lempel. Selecting the stories entailed long and intense discussions. For the translation phase of the project, we began by dividing the stories between us. For each story, one of us would produce an initial draft and the other would respond with line-by-line comments, questions, and suggestions.

Throughout her long career, Lempel never stopped wanting to reach out to English-language readers. It is a joy now to help fulfill that dream.

Ellen Cassedy
Yermiyahu Ahron Taub

ABOUT THE TRANSLATORS

Ellen Cassedy's translations appear in *Beautiful as the Moon, Radiant as the Stars: Jewish Women in Yiddish Stories*. With Yermiyahu Ahron Taub, she was the winner of the 2012 Translation Prize awarded by the Yiddish Book Center. She is the author of the award-winning *We Are Here: Memories of the Lithuanian Holocaust*. Visit her website at www.ellencassedy.com.

Yermiyahu Ahron Taub is the author of four books of poetry, including most recently *Prayers of a Heretic / Tfiles fun an apikoyres* (2013). *Tsugreytndik zikh tsu tantsn: naye yidishe lider / Preparing to Dance: New Yiddish Songs*, a CD of nine of his Yiddish poems set to music, was released in 2014. He was honored by the Museum of Jewish Heritage as one of New York's best emerging Jewish artists and has been nominated four times for a Pushcart Prize and twice for a Best of the Net award. With Ellen Cassedy, he was the winner of the 2012 translation prize awarded by the Yiddish Book Center. Visit his website at www.yataub.net.